CODENAME VISION

FILIP FORSBERG

1

Rome, Italy

The warm breeze caressed Dr. Claire Rossi's skin as she stepped into the park, a welcome relief from the oppressive heat that had enveloped Rome earlier. The late afternoon sun still glowed intensely, but its grip on the city was slowly loosening. The past few weeks had seen temperatures soaring above the seasonal average, but Claire didn't mind. On the contrary, she embraced the warmth as though greeting an old friend.

With purposeful strides, she followed the paved path through the park. The scent of freshly cut grass and blooming jasmine filled the air, a delightful contrast to the city's usual fumes. In the distance, across the lush greenery, her workplace came into view—BioVita. The white building stood like a beacon of hope and innovation against the clear blue sky.

BioVita was a small yet ambitious company, employing just under twenty people housed on three floors of the imposing structure. For Claire, the past months had been a whirlwind of intense work and minimal rest. She had spent nearly fifteen hours a day within the lab's walls, driven by a mix of passion and compulsive dedication to her work.

The Genesis prototype she wore in her left eye was the first of its kind—a marvel of biomedical innovation. Unlike previous attempts, her team had succeeded in developing a system that seamlessly integrated with the body's own neural network. Powered by the body's bioelectric field, it was self-sustaining and stable. Its basic neuroprocessor was powerful enough to restore vision but limited enough to ensure complete safety.

But it was Prometheus, the new experimental prototype, that kept her awake at night. With a neuroprocessor ten times more powerful than Genesis, it unlocked possibilities previously confined to science fiction. It could not only restore vision but enhance it, amplify it, making the impossible possible. Yet, this power came at a cost. Prometheus required constant access to its main unit to maintain stability, and without the precise synchronization codes from that unit, its neural interface risked overloading the wearer's visual cortex. More work remained to make it fully independent.

Claire suddenly realized how little of the city's life she had experienced lately. She barely had time to dash home for a quick shower, grab something edible, and snatch a few hours of sleep before being drawn back to BioVita and its tantalizing puzzles. With a sigh of both exhaustion and determination, Claire set her gaze on her workplace. Despite her overwhelming fatigue, a thrill bubbled within her. She knew they were on the brink of a breakthrough, and the thought of what it could mean for humanity filled her with renewed energy. Picking up her pace, she hurried toward the lab and the challenges awaiting her there.

Barely twenty meters ahead, an elderly woman approached Claire with a small dog on a leash. Suddenly, the little dog spotted something in a nearby tree and bolted. The woman, caught off guard by the dog's sudden dash, lost her grip on the leash and called out in alarm.

"Rufus! Come back!"

The dog darted toward Claire, who instinctively reacted. As the small bundle of fur sped past her, she lunged forward and grabbed the trailing leash. Adrenaline surged through her veins as she stood upright, pleased with her quick response.

Turning toward the elderly woman, Claire offered a friendly smile, ready to hand over the runaway dog. But her smile quickly turned to surprise as the woman, her wrinkled face flushed with exertion and anger, stormed toward her, wagging a finger accusingly.

"What on earth are you doing?" the woman hissed, her voice trembling with indignation.

Still stunned by the unexpected reaction, Claire held up the leash, extending it toward the woman in a conciliatory gesture. "Here," she said cautiously, "I stopped your dog."

The elderly woman snorted disdainfully. "Yes, I can see that. But my little Rufus is very delicate. He's a sensitive creature and can't handle being frightened like that. You were much too rough!"

Claire blinked a few times, taken aback and unsure how to respond. The words felt clumsy in her mouth as she tried to explain. "I was only trying to help."

With a sharp glare, the woman leaned forward and yanked the leash from Claire's hand. In the same motion, she scooped up the still-barking Rufus, soothing him with a scratch behind his ears.

"I don't need help from people like you," the woman snapped. "You're lucky nothing happened to Rufus."

With that, the woman swept past Claire in a cloud of perfume and indignation, leaving her standing frozen in place. She suddenly felt drained, as though all her energy had been sapped. With a deep sigh, she shook her head slowly and murmured to herself,

"Well, thanks for the help."

A bitter taste spread in her mouth as the realization struck her— sometimes, no matter what you did, it was wrong. The sound of the woman's muttering and the dog's whining faded into the distance, leaving Claire alone with her thoughts and a gnawing sense of injustice.

She stood still for a few seconds, still shaken by the unexpected confrontation. With a resigned sigh, she shrugged and continued along the path through the park. The sound of rustling leaves and distant traffic blended with the determined rhythm of her steps on the pavement.

Reaching the edge of the park, she nimbly crossed Via Siracusa, adrenaline still coursing through her veins. She slipped between two parked cars, their glossy surfaces reflecting the afternoon sun, and hurried to the massive gate leading to the building housing BioVita.

With practiced ease, Claire pulled out a key card from her inner pocket and swiped it across the black reader by the gate. A low hum was followed by a distinct click as the heavy metal lock released. She quickly passed through, ensuring the gate closed securely behind her.

Inside, another security barrier awaited. Claire navigated it with the same precision before beginning her ascent up the stairs. Her footsteps echoed lightly in the quiet stairwell, a reminder of the building's age and history.

Finally, she reached a third door. A discreet plaque proclaimed "BioVita" in elegant lettering. Beside the door was a dark screen, and Claire unhesitatingly placed her left hand on its surface. A bright green line scanned her palm with a faint hum. After a few seconds of tense silence, a synthetic voice announced, "Welcome, Dr. Rossi."

The door slid open silently, and Claire stepped into BioVita's heart—a beautiful old apartment skillfully transformed into a state-of-the-art laboratory. Three of the large rooms were encased in thick, bulletproof glass. Inside, advanced medical equipment blinked and whirred. Eight or nine people in crisp white coats moved purposefully between workstations, deeply focused on their tasks.

Claire passed these rooms and headed toward the innermost two. In the far room, two people sat around a massive dark wooden desk. At the center of the desk stood a glass container with metal edges and a black battery mounted on its side, seemingly unremarkable but holding contents that could change the world.

A pear-shaped man with a receding hairline and a face full of character looked up as Claire entered. His eyes shone with excitement and relief.

"There you are, Claire. Good to see you back," he said warmly. Claire couldn't help but laugh, the tension from earlier melting away in the familiar surroundings. "Luca, I was only gone six hours. What we've created here won't run away, will it?"

A middle-aged woman with neatly pinned gray-streaked hair reached out and grasped Claire's hand. Her touch was warm and brimming with enthusiasm. "But isn't it incredible, what we've created? Or rather, what *you* have created."

Claire returned the handshake as she pulled out a chair and sank into it with a soft sigh. "It is, Maria. It really is. The possibilities with this are so vast I don't even know where to start. This is something unique in the history of the world."

Luca shifted his gaze from Claire to the glass container on the desk. The container, barely twenty centimeters tall and eight centimeters in diameter, was a masterpiece of precision-engineered titanium alloy and quantum-enhanced glass. It was filled with a clear, faintly blue liquid—a specially developed cryogenic solution that both stabilized and nourished its precious cargo. Tiny bubbles of purified oxygen rose slowly through the liquid in a mesmerizing pattern.

But it wasn't the container that was exceptional; it was what lay within. Suspended in the liquid, held in place by an almost invisible network of nanofibers, floated a fully functional artificial eye—Prometheus. At first glance, it was nearly indistinguishable from a human organ—the perfectly shaped sphere, the crystal-clear cornea, the intricate blood vessels spidering across the pristine white sclera. Yet, upon closer inspection, subtle details revealed its true nature.

The iris was a fascinating blend of deep blue and emerald green, with microscopic etchings that caught the light in complex patterns. Beneath the surface, a faint blue glow pulsed in time with the prototype's neuroprocessor. The jet-black pupil seemed almost alive, expanding and contracting in response to changes in ambient light. Through the transparent cornea, the advanced biomimetic systems were visible—a perfect synthesis of organic tissue and quantum technology.

Around the base of the container, a series of sophisticated diagnostic displays monitored everything from the liquid temperature to neural activity patterns. Small LED indicators pulsed green and blue, confirming all systems were functioning optimally. A discreet control unit on the side regulated the delicate power supply keeping the prototype alive.

What was most fascinating was how the eye seemed to react to its surroundings—small, almost imperceptible movements and shifts in the blue glow suggested a form of awareness. It was neither wholly artificial nor wholly organic but something in between—a scientific miracle teetering on the edge of technology and life.

"Think of the possibilities this will unlock," Luca murmured, his voice filled with reverence and anticipation.

None of them in the room realized that, at that very moment, two dark vans were pulling up along Via Siracusa, stopping in front of the gate below. The sound of car doors opening and closing was drowned out by the city's hum, as men in dark suits moved swiftly and silently toward the building.

2

Rome, Italy

Inside the rear of the second dark van, Gavrail Zaytsev took a deep, measured breath. Slowly exhaling, he felt his pulse steady as the familiar rhythm of pre-mission adrenaline coursed through his veins. No matter how many operations he undertook, each one felt as significant as his first.

His reflection flitted across the window—a man just over forty, with short, dark hair peppered with steel gray at the temples, adding an air of authority. Time had been kind to Gavrail; through relentless discipline, he had kept his body in peak condition, strong and agile like a man half his age. In his line of work, such readiness was not optional—every mission could be his last.

Aside from the silent, focused driver, two other men shared the van. Both wore identical black outfits to Gavrail's—discreet yet practical. One of them, Marco, withdrew a firearm from a concealed holster under his jacket. With practiced hands, he checked the mechanism before sliding it back into place with a barely audible click.

"So, Gavrail," Marco said, his voice low and controlled, "you're leading this one. Any final instructions?"

Gavrail's mouth set into a tight line. This operation was a departure from his usual solo missions. Normally, he worked alone, acquiring his target and making it disappear without a trace. But for this specific mission, he had been hired to lead a team of handpicked mercenaries in a precision strike on a company nestled in the heart of Rome.

"No," Gavrail replied after a brief pause, his tone steady and commanding. "We've covered everything. You and Nico handle the gate as quickly and quietly as possible. Then we leave two

men from the second team at the entrance for security while
the rest of us head up to BioVita."
He let his gaze pass over the men in the van. "We've got the
access cards we need, and with only a group of researchers
inside, this should go smoothly."
The air in the van was thick with anticipation. Gavrail felt the
adrenaline intensify, sharpening his senses to a razor's edge. He
closed his eyes momentarily, visualizing the mission in precise
detail. When he opened them again, his steel-hard gaze revealed
a man fully prepared for the task at hand.
"Let's move. On my command," he said, his voice cutting
through the tension like a blade as he spoke into a walkie-talkie
retrieved from a bag at his feet.
With those words, the operation sprang into motion, the air
practically crackling with electric anticipation.
The driver eased the van onto the street leading to their target.
The morning air in Rome was heavy with exhaust fumes and the
tantalizing aroma of freshly baked bread from nearby bakeries.
Though traffic was light at this hour, Rome was a city that never
truly slept, always alive with movement. People strolled along
the sidewalks, their laughter and chatter blending with the hum
of engines, blissfully unaware of the drama about to unfold.
As the van maneuvered around a stationary delivery truck
belching diesel fumes, the two dark vehicles approached their
destination. The venerable facade of the BioVita building
loomed ahead, bathed in the yellow glow of streetlights.
Gavrail's sharp eyes scanned the surroundings through the
tinted windows. Two women passed by in animated
conversation, their high heels clicking against the pavement. A
man walked his dog, the leash rattling faintly before they
vanished from view.
Satisfied with his assessment, Gavrail pressed the walkie-talkie
to his lips. "Go," he muttered, his voice low yet infused with the
authority that made his men tense in readiness.
Marco swung the van's door open, the metal creaking softly
under his firm grip. The three men exited with precision, their
black-clad forms blending seamlessly into the shadows. Gavrail

slid the door shut behind him with a muffled thud that echoed faintly on the quiet street. From the second van, three more figures emerged, moving as silently as predators. The six-man team advanced toward the gate, where a discreet sign read "BioVita" in silver lettering.

Without a word, Nico and Marco took their positions at the gate, their breaths steady and measured. Marco pulled out what might appear to the untrained eye to be a simple tool but was, in reality, a sophisticated lock-picking device. Illegal for civilians but invaluable in the hands of professionals like them. Marco knelt, inserted the device into the gate's lock, and activated it in quick succession. The sound was barely perceptible, but to Gavrail, it was like thunder in the tense silence.

Fifteen nerve-wracking seconds later, a distinct click signaled success. The gate swung open soundlessly.

Gavrail nudged it further with a decisive motion, gesturing for two men to remain as guards. His expression was grim, his body coiled like a spring. The remaining team slipped inside the dim corridor, their movements catlike and quiet. The scent of disinfectant and aged electronics greeted them—a stark reminder of the building's scientific purpose.

At the next door, the procedure repeated, equally efficient. They climbed the stairs quickly but cautiously, their soles rasping softly against the concrete.

At the final massive door, they faced a new challenge—this one impervious to the lock-picking device. But Gavrail was prepared. His face a mask of concentration, he unrolled a thin plastic sheet no larger than a palm. With surgical precision, he pressed it against the black scanner beside the door.

He placed his hand on the sheet, his heart pounding as a green laser scanned the surface with a hum that seemed deafening in the stillness.

A synthetic voice broke the silence. "Welcome, Dr. Rossi." The words hung in the air, a final warning.

The door opened with a muted click, and Gavrail's pulse quickened as adrenaline surged through his veins. They were in. Now the real mission began.

With a nod to his men, whose eyes glinted with determination in the dim light, he stepped into BioVita's inner sanctum. The air was cool and sterile, carrying the faint mingling scents of chemicals and electronics. Gavrail inhaled deeply, prepared to seize what they had come for—no matter the cost.

His fingers tightened around the weapon at his side, a silent reminder of the stakes as he led his team into the heart of BioVita's domain.

3

Rome, Italy

Dr. Claire Rossi felt a wave of satisfaction wash over her as she gazed at the small cryogenic glass container in front of her. The clinical scent of disinfectant mingled with the bitter aroma of coffee grounds from the morning's first cup, a smell that had become a familiar companion during the long nights in the lab. The faint blue glow from the Prometheus prototype flickered across the container's surface, casting ghostly shadows on the walls, as if emphasizing the miracle resting within. That they had managed to create a second, improved version felt almost surreal after so many setbacks.

The prickling discomfort in her left eye reminded her of the price of success, but she ignored it, as she had ignored so many sacrifices along the way. Endless days and nights, when the darkness outside the windows blurred with the first rays of dawn, had pushed them to their limits. And now, finally, they had created a version capable of mass production.

A laugh bubbled up inside her, filled with both relief and triumph, echoing against the lab's bare walls. With trembling hands, she reached out to Luca and Maria, her closest colleagues and friends throughout this exhausting journey. The warmth of their hands against hers felt like a physical affirmation of their shared achievement—a reminder that this was not just another fevered dream born of exhaustion.

"Thank you for staying with me through it all," she said, her voice thick with emotion as she struggled against the recurring haze in her left eye. "Thank you for not giving up."

Maria's eyes shimmered with unshed tears, and her smile lit up her entire face as she squeezed Claire's hand. "You know we never would," she replied softly but firmly. "Not after everything we learned from the first prototype."

Maria took a deep breath, her brow furrowing in thought. "There are over forty million blind people in the world," she said, her voice quivering slightly with suppressed emotion. "Once we solve the final issues with Prometheus, we can finally give them hope. Even if we only help a fraction of them... that's still millions of lives we can change. It's... it's almost overwhelming to think about."

Claire rose unsteadily and moved to the open window, her thoughts whirling. A faint resonance caused her vision to flicker momentarily, like static on an old TV screen. The city lights twinkled outside like countless tiny stars, a reminder of the world beyond the lab and everything they had fought for. Memories of her grandfather, blind for many years, surfaced unbidden. His smile and the gentle hands that brushed over her face to "see" her with his fingertips filled her with a wave of tenderness and renewed resolve. His struggle had planted the seed of her life's work, which had grown into an obsession to help the blind.

Placing her hands on the cold metal window frame, she leaned forward. The evening air wafting through the half-open window carried the distinct scent of autumn—a blend of damp asphalt and withered leaves. The priority now was to make Prometheus accessible in a way that could help the maximum number of people without becoming prohibitively expensive. A maze of ethical, economic, and logistical challenges awaited, but she had deliberately deferred those thoughts. Now, she could avoid them no longer.

Her gaze drifted down to the street below, where two dark vans were parked directly in front of BioVita's main entrance. They seemed out of place in the orderly business park, like two dark stains on an otherwise pristine canvas. A creeping sense of unease slithered up her spine, an instinctive reaction to something that felt off. The blue glow from the prototype in its container seemed to pulse stronger for a moment, as if responding to her growing apprehension.

Claire drummed her fingers nervously on the windowsill, her brow furrowing. A throbbing ache began to build behind her left eye, more intense than before. The metallic taste of fear spread in her mouth.

"Are we expecting a delivery?" she asked, her voice thick with confusion and rising concern.

Before anyone could answer, a scream tore through the air from the hallway outside—a sharp, piercing sound filled with raw panic. The noise shattered the lab's tranquil atmosphere like a blade slicing through fabric. Claire froze, every muscle in her body coiled like a spring as adrenaline flooded her veins. In the brief, shocked silence that followed, she could hear her own heart pounding wildly in her chest, a drumbeat warning of imminent danger. Something was terribly wrong, and she realized with chilling clarity that their moment of triumph was about to turn into a nightmare.

With trembling hands, she pointed to the glass container housing Prometheus, its blue glow now pulsing like an agitated heartbeat.

"Luca!" Her voice cracked with desperation. "Get Prometheus into the safe! Now!"

The sound of hurried footsteps echoed through the hallway, growing louder with each passing second. Metallic thuds and muffled screams mingled with the crash of shattered glass. Claire could feel panic rising in her chest like a tidal wave, threatening to drown her rational thought. Yet somewhere deep within, she found a core of strength, forged by years of setbacks and hardships.

They would not take Prometheus. Not now. Not after everything they had sacrificed.

Her jaw clenched, and she turned to Luca and Maria, who were already scrambling to secure the prototype. Whatever was coming, Claire knew one thing for certain—they would not go down without a fight.

4

Rome, Italy

Gavrail raised his weapon, the cold metal an extension of his will, and took a determined step into the hallway. The scent of disinfectant and sterile air struck him, a sharp contrast to the crisp afternoon air outside. To his left were large rooms enclosed by glass walls, with a central space visible through the transparent barriers. Light from overhead lamps reflected off the glass, creating an almost ghostly ambiance.

A few white-clad figures with face masks looked up in startled surprise from their work, their eyes widening behind protective goggles as they stared at the black-clad men storming into their workspace. Their latex-covered hands froze mid-motion above microscopes and test tubes.

Gavrail nodded to Marco.

"Check them," he said, his voice as cold and sharp as a blade.

Marco didn't hesitate. With purposeful strides, he approached the glass door that marked the entrance to the lab. His breathing was measured, his pulse steady despite the intensity of the moment. He grasped the handle and pressed it down smoothly. The door clicked, the sound unnervingly loud in the tense silence. As he pushed it open, a faint hissing noise accompanied the release of the lab's pressurized air.

One of the white-clad figures raised their hands in protest, their voice trembling as words spilled out. "No! What are you doing? You can't just—"

Marco moved with practiced fluidity, lifting his pistol and aiming directly at the figure's face. His eyes were ice.

"Quiet," he commanded. "Take off your mask."

The figure hesitated for what felt like an eternity. Marco lowered his aim toward the floor and squeezed the trigger. The weapon barked sharply, and the bullet struck the ground with an ear-splitting crack, making everyone in the room jump.

The figure needed no further encouragement, fumbling to remove their mask. A woman's pale face emerged, her eyes wide with terror, sweat beading on her forehead.

"Please," she pleaded, her voice hoarse. "I have two children at home. Please."

Marco was unmoved by her desperation. His question came quick and cutting: "Are you Dr. Rossi?"

The woman shook her head frantically, her hair flying around her face. "No, no," she stammered.

"Where is she?"

Her gaze darted between Marco and the others in the room, fear warring with self-preservation. Finally, survival instincts won out. "She's in the large conference room," she answered, voice trembling.

"Where's that?"

"Down the hall, to the right," the woman blurted, her words tumbling over one another in her haste to comply.

Marco pivoted, his movements precise and controlled. "She's down the hall, to the right," he reported.

Gavrail's face was a mask of stone. Without a word, he nodded at Luca, and the two advanced purposefully. They passed another glass-enclosed room where three white-clad figures stood frozen, staring helplessly at the intruders.

The tension in the air was palpable. Every step Gavrail and Luca took echoed down the corridor, a countdown to the inevitable confrontation. Their dark silhouettes reflected in the gleaming surfaces around them, like shadows stalking through this sterile world of science and discovery.

Finally, they reached a glass door marked **Conference Room**. Gavrail's heartbeat thrummed in his ears as he pushed it open. Inside, three people—two women and a man—instinctively raised their hands in surrender. The sharp, metallic tang of fear permeated the room.

Gavrail entered slowly, his weapon raised. Luca followed close behind, his weapon also ready. Their black attire absorbed the light, rendering them living shadows in the sterile environment.

The three individuals stared at the gun as if it were an alien artifact, their eyes wide with terror. For a fleeting moment, Gavrail felt invincible, power coursing through his veins.

"Dr. Claire Rossi?" His voice was low and controlled, yet sharp enough to cut through the silence.

The woman on the far left blinked—a reflex Gavrail's trained eye didn't miss. He turned toward her, his weapon tracking with precision.

"You must be Dr. Rossi."

A few seconds stretched out like an eternity. Outside, a distant ambulance siren wailed, a grimly ironic reminder of the danger in the room. Slowly, the woman nodded, her eyes fixed on the weapon in his hand.

"Yes, I'm Dr. Rossi." Her voice was steady despite the situation. Gavrail forced a smile.

"Excellent. I'm here for something you have. If I get it without complications, you and your colleagues will walk out of here unharmed. You have my word. Do you understand?"

Claire's face was pale, her breathing erratic, but her eyes burned with a defiant intensity.

"Yes," she whispered.

Gavrail lowered the gun slightly.

"Claire, listen to me. You need to take a few deep breaths, understand? This won't work if you faint. So, I need you to sit down, alright?"

Claire hesitated but then complied.

"Alright," she said, sinking into a chair, her back ramrod straight.

"Good," Gavrail continued. "I assume you understand why my colleagues and I are here."

"I have an idea," Claire replied, her voice steadier now.

"Excellent! That saves us a lot of trouble. I gather you're as smart as your dossier suggests. So, if you'd kindly hand over *Prometheus' Eye,* we'll vanish as quickly as we appeared."

Claire stared at Gavrail, her expression difficult to read. Fear radiated from her, perhaps even terror, but there was something else—a flicker of defiance, an ember of resistance that refused to die.

Five long seconds passed. Claire inhaled deeply.

"No," she said, her voice soft but resolute.

At first, Gavrail didn't register the word, its improbability hanging in the charged air. When realization struck, rage surged within him, hot and suffocating. Slowly, he raised the gun, aiming it at her.

"Excuse me?" His voice was dangerously calm, the stillness before a storm.

Some color returned to Claire's face as she straightened slightly in her chair.

"I said no," she repeated, each word deliberate.

"You're making a grave mistake, Dr. Rossi," Gavrail said, his voice now hard as steel. "You should know—we know everything about what goes on here."

"It very well might be," Claire said, her eyes blazing with determination, "but you'll never get the Eye. Not in a million years."

Gavrail bit his tongue, his gaze locked on hers. He blinked a couple of times before shifting his weapon to aim at the second woman. "If you don't hand it over, your colleague will die."

The older woman stood rigid, defiance etched into her features, and Gavrail felt a sting of frustration. *Damn these Italian women,* he thought bitterly.

"I'll give you five seconds. Five. Four." His voice was flat, emotionless.

Both women glared at him defiantly, and a flicker of doubt crept into his mind. This wasn't going according to plan.

"Three. Two—"

The overweight, balding man in the middle suddenly dropped to his knees, his face contorted with fear. "Stop! For God's sake, stop!"

Claire turned on him with a fiery glare. "Luca! No, be quiet!" Her voice was a mixture of despair and betrayal.

Encouraged by the man's capitulation, Gavrail took a step forward. "You're doing the right thing, Luca. Give me Prometheus, and this all ends."

With a deep, shuddering sob, Luca rose shakily to his feet and pointed with a trembling hand toward a painting on the far wall. "There. In the safe," he said, his voice breaking with shame.

Gavrail nodded toward the painting. "Get it out," he ordered.

Head bowed, Luca shuffled over to the painting, slid it aside, and opened the safe behind it. Reaching in with both hands, he carefully removed something that resembled a glass container. He carried it back, setting it gently on the table in front of them.

"Here it is—Prometheus' Eye. The battery in its mobile container lasts just over 48 hours, no more. Now, please, let us go." Luca's voice was barely more than a whisper, a prayer for mercy.

A cold smile spread across Gavrail's face.

"Thank you, Dr. Rossi. But I'm afraid that's not all. You're coming with us, too. We're taking both Prometheus and you."

He raised his weapon toward Luca, but in the same instant, Claire lunged backward. Her chair crashed to the floor with a deafening clatter, and before anyone could react, she hurled herself at the window. The glass shattered into a thousand sparkling fragments, exploding outward into the afternoon light. The sharp sound of breaking glass was immediately followed by gunshots, echoing through the room.

Gavrail moved with mechanical precision, firing two shots in rapid succession. The sound reverberated through the sterile lab like thunderclaps, gunpowder mingling with the antiseptic smell of disinfectant. He rushed to the broken window, where cold night air rushed in, carrying the distant wail of sirens. Glass crunched beneath his boots as he leaned out, scanning the parking lot below with trained eyes.

Three stories down, he spotted Claire limping between parked cars. Her white lab coat glowed in the darkness like a ghost, now marred with dark red stains from the glass shards. The approaching sirens grew louder, their echoes bouncing off the buildings.

"Damn it!" Gavrail hissed through gritted teeth as he activated his radio. His voice was tight with frustration as he reported, "The target is fleeing! She exited through a window on the south side. Stop her!"

The suffocating silence that followed was broken only by the monotonous dripping of blood and the crunch of shattered glass underfoot. Gavrail's breathing was steady as he turned back to the glass container still on the lab bench. The advanced prototype rested in its custom-designed cradle—a device no larger than the palm of a hand. Its surface gleamed with intricate cooling systems and diagnostic displays, casting an eerie blue glow across the room. A small indicator pulsed rhythmically, like an artificial heartbeat, confirming that the portable power supply was functioning.

Time was slipping away. Gavrail was painfully aware of the countdown. He had memorized every detail of Dr. Rossi's technical documentation, provided by the Shadow Council's spy at BioVita. Without the stabilizing quantum matrix in the main unit, they had only 48 hours before the prototype's advanced processor began losing its precise calibration. Prometheus' neuroprocessor was like a delicate orchestra—it demanded perfect synchronization with its host. Without the correct calibration codes, neural integration would be a deadly gamble. With meticulous precision, he secured the cradle in its specially designed case. The digital display on the case began an unrelenting countdown: **47:58:23**. The crimson digits glowed like a grim reminder of their narrow window.

Gavrail drew a deep, controlled breath, his eyes scanning the room one final time. Behind him lay two lifeless bodies sprawled on the polished floor, casualties of science and greed. But the third—the critical piece in this twisted game—had managed to slip through his grasp.

When he spoke into the radio again, his voice was as cold as winter steel.

"All units, prioritize finding Rossi. She's injured and won't have gone far." He paused, his gaze following the trail of blood leading toward the stairwell, his mind racing.

"Or wait—never mind. We need to vanish before the police arrive."

5

Malmoe, Sweden

The traffic light's sharp red-yellow glow cut through the twilight before switching to green. Hugo Xavier let his black Audi glide forward, turning right just as a dark shadow appeared out of nowhere. A man on a bicycle, dressed entirely in black, almost collided with the car's front. Hugo slammed on the brakes, the ABS vibrating underfoot as the tires screeched against the asphalt. The cyclist, balancing a phone between his shoulder and ear, swerved at the last moment, shouting something unintelligible through the closed car window.

Hugo shook his head slowly, his heart pounding as it returned to a steadier rhythm.

"What an idiot," he muttered, gripping the steering wheel tighter.

The chilly October afternoon was giving way to evening as Hugo passed the bus stop at Södervärn. Streetlights cast a yellowish glow over a few bundled-up commuters, their collars turned against the biting wind. At the next intersection, he turned right again, heading into the expansive hospital complex. The sun had sunk below the horizon, leaving behind a violet sky that deepened with each passing moment. Long shadows from the towering hospital buildings stretched across the asphalt as he steered toward the parking garage.

After parking, he took a deep breath, already catching the distinct hospital smell—a mix of disinfectant and something metallic—that always made him slightly queasy. It was just before five o'clock when he reached the automatic glass doors of the hospital entrance. They slid open with a muted hiss, and he paused under the fluorescent lights to study the orientation board.

"Fourth floor," he murmured, striding toward the elevators.

The elevator's smooth ascent was punctuated by a soft *ding* as it reached the fourth floor. When the doors slid open, he was greeted by a large, sterile hallway marking the department's entrance. A woman in a tailored dark suit stood at attention, her sharp posture radiating authority. Her piercing gaze tracked his every move as Hugo stepped out of the elevator.

"Hugo Xavier. Novus," he introduced himself confidently.

The woman stepped forward, her expression professionally neutral.

"Do you have identification?" Her tone was firm but polite.

Hugo offered a polite smile, nodding toward his jacket pocket.

"Yes, may I retrieve it?"

"Slowly."

Moving deliberately, Hugo unbuttoned his navy coat and pulled out his wallet. The woman scrutinized his ID card for what felt like an eternity before finally nodding.

"Thank you," she said, handing it back. "How can I help you?"

"I'm here to see Madeleine Singh," Hugo replied, a faint tension creeping into his chest as he said his boss's name.

"Do you have an appointment?" Her tone remained strictly professional.

"Yes, she's expecting me." He flashed a warm smile. "In fact, she asked me to come. And when the boss says jump, you don't keep her waiting, right?" He added a wink, attempting to lighten the mood.

The woman remained unimpressed, merely nodding toward a heavy metal door behind her.

"At the end of the hall. I'll notify the inner guard that you're coming."

"Thank you," Hugo said, giving her a thumbs-up.

With a swipe of her access card and the press of a button, the massive door opened with a low rumble.

The corridor beyond was long and clinically white, the pervasive scent of disinfectant mingling with the sterile tang of medicine. The low hum of the air conditioning was broken only by the muffled sound of his footsteps on the polished floor. At the far end, a uniformed guard rose from a desk as Hugo approached.

"Wait," the guard said, raising a hand.

Hugo frowned, his shoulders tensing.

"Madeleine is expecting me."

The guard gave a strained smile.

"That's fine. I just need to check if she's awake. One moment."

As the guard disappeared through another door, Hugo stood in silence, listening to the faint beeping of medical equipment somewhere nearby. His thoughts drifted to the recent mission— the moment they had finally located Madeleine... He shook his head, clearing his mind, as the guard returned and held the door open.

"Go ahead."

The room Hugo entered was unexpectedly cozy for a hospital ward. A large bed dominated one side, a flat-screen TV mounted on the wall opposite. Two comfortable-looking armchairs were positioned by the window, where soft evening light filtered through the blinds, casting gentle shadows across the walls. His quiet steps on the linoleum floor disrupted the stillness as he approached the bed.

Under the crisp white hospital sheets, a figure stirred, and when the blanket shifted, Hugo found himself locked in the intense gaze of Madeleine Singh.

"Hugo," she said, her voice weaker than he was accustomed to hearing from his normally commanding boss.

Hugo approached carefully, taking her hand in his. The warmth of her skin reassured him—a sign of life and strength, despite the circumstances. He leaned forward, pressing a light kiss to her forehead, noticing the faint scent of hospital soap clinging to her. Her face bore signs of exhaustion, with new lines etching her cheeks and chin. Yet her eyes—sharp, intelligent, and unyielding—remained unchanged, meeting his with unwavering intensity.

"How are you?" he asked gently, his tone softer than usual, devoid of the command or sharpness it often carried in the field.

Madeleine smacked her lips.

"This has been the longest week of my life." She shot an irritated glance at the IV stand beside her bed. "Can you imagine how boring it is to lie here day after day?"

Hugo chuckled warmly, lowering himself onto the edge of the bed with care, mindful of the cables and tubes surrounding her. The bed creaked slightly under his weight.

"I can imagine, boss," he said, his eyes flicking over the monitoring equipment pulsing with a soft green glow. "But maybe it's not the worst thing. After everything that happened on the last mission, maybe some rest isn't such a bad idea."

"Rest?" Madeleine's voice cut through the room with sudden sharpness. "This isn't rest. And after what happened on the last mission, the *last* thing I need is to be lying here."

Hugo grimaced, running a hand over the stubble on his chin as he scratched it thoughtfully. A heavy silence settled between them, broken only by the rhythmic beeping of the heart monitor. He knew exactly what Madeleine was referring to— memories of the last mission were still raw and painful.

For two years, Novus had been targeted by two brutal attacks. Dedicated employees had lost their lives in service to the company—lives extinguished far too soon. And Madeleine herself... His jaw clenched as he recalled how close it had been. The kidnapping had been meticulously executed, and without the seamless coordination of his team, they would never have found and rescued her in time.

Despite her age, Madeleine had shown incredible mental fortitude. She had fought, survived, and against all odds, made it back. The mission itself had been a blend of success and failure, but that was secondary. What mattered was that Madeleine was alive and on the path to recovery. All it required now was time, rest, and patience—the last of which seemed the hardest for his energetic boss.

Suddenly, a spark lit up Madeleine's eyes as she caught his gaze, and Hugo recognized the look. That intense, piercing expression always meant one thing: something important was on her mind.

"Alright, Hugo, talk to me."

Her tone carried an undercurrent of authority, and Hugo instinctively straightened on the bed's edge. This was no longer a friendly visit—this was a meeting with his boss, no matter the setting.

6

Malmoe, Sweden

Hugo slowly ran a hand over his chin, feeling the rough stubble scrape against his palm. His reflection passed fleetingly in the mirror by the sink—a tall, broad-shouldered man whose presence seemed to fill the room. His closely cropped dark hair and three days of beard growth lent him a rugged air, further accentuated by his chiseled features. His dark eyes caught the glimmer of headlights from a passing car, the light momentarily casting dramatic shadows across his face before the room was plunged back into darkness.

"I've gone through all the material with Fredrika," he began, his deep voice steady. "The staff has been sent home. Officially, it's because the building needs repairs after the damage caused by Malaconda's men." He paused, a wry smile tugging at his lips. "Which, I suppose, is true enough."

Madeleine shifted, propping herself into a more upright position. The hospital bed creaked softly under the strain. "So, what's your take on all this? After all, it was your idea that there's a mole in Novus—that's why our last mission failed."

Hugo's gaze hardened, turning cold. "Yes. In my opinion, there are too many unanswered questions about what happened during the attack. It doesn't add up." His jaw tensed as he continued. "We've implemented every precaution since the first assault. Cameras installed everywhere, entry cards meticulously tracked, and even the encrypted code designed to protect the system from external breaches." He paused, letting the weight of his words sink in. "And yet, despite all that, an attack team gets in, bypasses our defenses, and kidnaps you. Call it what you want, but from where I stand, the only way something like that could succeed is if someone on the inside is working against us."

A shadow of sorrow passed over Madeleine's face, aging her further. "You can't imagine what it feels like to build something great, only to watch it crumble beyond your control. The frustration is... unbearable."

Hugo nodded slowly, the gravity of her words pressing down on him. "No, I can only imagine."

The silence that followed was heavy, punctuated only by the muffled sounds of distant traffic and the persistent hum of the air conditioning. Madeleine brushed a stray lock of hair from her face, her eyes lifting to meet his. A quiet fire burned within them, and for a moment, Hugo saw the extraordinary strength that had carried Madeleine to the pinnacle of the security industry.

"Hugo, you know as well as I do that it has to be true," she said, her voice low but intense. "There is a traitor within Novus. It's the only explanation for why our defenses were so ineffective." She gripped the bed's edge tightly, her knuckles white. "But this isn't just about finding a mole anymore. This is so much bigger now. Considering our reputation in the industry and how hard we fought to recover after the first attack..." She swallowed hard. "To be targeted again—by the same organization, no less—this is a devastating blow."

Hugo bit his lower lip, his thoughts swirling like autumn leaves in a storm. His gaze drifted to the window, where the city lights twinkled in the night. Novus operated in the shadowy space between the legal and the illicit, a gray zone that surrounded the modern corporate world. Over the past decade, major international corporations had increasingly turned to discreet resources like Novus to resolve their problems—be it industrial espionage, safeguarding trade secrets, or more extreme measures like kidnappings and, in dire cases, assassinations. In today's high-stakes business climate, with astronomical sums at stake, some were willing to take drastic measures to settle disputes. It was in this twilight world that Novus had risen to prominence, earning a reputation as a trusted provider of services that corporations needed to survive.

Turning back to Madeleine, he nodded heavily. "Our reputation isn't in the best shape right now, no."

"Exactly." Madeleine's voice cut through the room like a scalpel. "And you know as well as I do that in our line of work, reputation is everything." She leaned forward, ignoring the discomfort the movement caused her. "If we don't fix this quickly, I don't know if Novus has a future."

Hugo sat in silence, listening to the distant wail of an ambulance siren echoing between the buildings outside.

"What do you want me to do?" His voice was barely above a whisper.

The fire in Madeleine's eyes flared with renewed intensity. "For now, you and Fredrika have full authority to do whatever it takes to uncover the traitor." Her grip on his hand tightened. "You are two of my most trusted people. There is no one else I'd entrust with this." She paused, drawing a deep breath. "And I know I need to stay here for a while longer. There's no point in me rushing after a mole while I'm not fully recovered—I'd only risk making things worse."

Hugo opened his mouth to respond, but she raised a hand, cutting him off. Her voice was firm as she continued. "I'm giving you access to the master codes. They'll open every Novus database—codes that only I have access to. I've already spoken to Fredrika and told her the same thing I'm telling you now." She paused again, letting her words sink in. "I need your help, Hugo. Help me save Novus."

The weight of her plea hung heavy in the room. Hugo sat motionless, processing the magnitude of her words and the trust she had placed in him. Finally, he took her hand, squeezing it gently yet firmly, and met her intense gaze with one of equal resolve.

"I promise, Madeleine," he said, his voice steady and brimming with determination. "I'll do everything I can."

In the dim light of the bedside lamp, he saw a single tear slide down Madeleine's cheek—a rare glimpse of vulnerability in a woman otherwise defined by her unwavering strength.

7

Malmoe, Sweden

The flickering candlelight danced across Lita Marquesz's olive-toned skin, making her eyes glimmer like dark jewels in the dim room. She smiled, a row of pearl-white teeth catching the warm glow. The seductive aroma of fine red wine mingled with her subtle perfume as Hugo Xavier leaned in to plant a gentle kiss on her cheek.

"You know you're my everything, don't you?" he said softly, his voice barely above a whisper.

Lita blinked playfully, tossing her head so that her luscious, raven-black curls tumbled over her shoulders like a cascade.

"You always know the right things to say, Hugo. You always have," she replied, her Spanish accent adding a musical lilt to her words.

A smile spread across Hugo's face as he lifted his glass of wine, swirling the ruby liquid thoughtfully before taking a measured sip. The ambiance of Rådhuskällaren, one of Malmö's most esteemed restaurants, enveloped them in timeless elegance. The chandeliers above cast a muted glow over the crisp white linens and polished silverware. He felt a surge of gratitude that the babysitter had been able to step in at such short notice to care for Elektra. He needed this moment with Lita, a reprieve before the storm he knew was coming.

The aftermath of the recent mission had been impossible to ignore—someone within Novus was leaking information to their enemies. The thought of a traitor made his jaw clench.

Madeleine's kidnapping had made the truth inescapably clear. Accepting that someone in the organization was working against them felt like poison on his tongue, but there was no other plausible explanation. Action was now imperative. Under the guise of renovations, almost all employees had been sent home, though the true purpose was to flush out the mole—at any cost. He reached out and gently brushed a stray curl from Lita's cheek. As he looked at her, he was reminded once again of how lucky he was. His wife was the embodiment of classic Spanish beauty, with a magnetic presence that turned heads wherever she went.

"Lita, something's happened at work," he said.

Her smile faltered for a brief moment before she regained her composure. Leaning back in her antique wooden chair, her wine glass balanced between her slender fingers, she met his gaze with her almond-shaped eyes.

"Ah, so that's why you wanted to take me out to dinner," she said with a touch of resignation, the hint of it cutting into Hugo like a dagger.

He forced a playful tone into his voice as he lied. "No, not at all. I don't need a reason to take my wife out, do I?"

The seconds crawled by in a heavy silence. A discreet waiter in a pristine white shirt and black vest approached their table, quietly refilling their crystal water glasses.

"Is everything to your satisfaction?" the waiter asked in a hushed tone.

"Everything's fine, thank you," Hugo replied quickly, eager to be alone with Lita again.

The waiter nodded professionally and disappeared between the tables as silently as he had come.

Hugo reached across the table, taking Lita's hand in his, feeling the warmth of her skin against his palm.

"Listen, sweetheart. I can't say much right now, but there's a situation at work. I'll need to be away for a few days until it's resolved."

"Is it a mission? Are you leaving?" The worry in her voice was subtle but palpable, an undercurrent Hugo had come to recognize well—the ever-present concern that came with his line of work.

"No, it's not a mission, exactly," he reassured her, stroking the back of her hand with his thumb. "It's more of a...special situation that's come up. Madeleine and I have agreed that I need to handle it."

Lita frowned slightly, crossing her arms over her chest—a familiar gesture that signaled her discontent.

"You're not an easy man to love, Hugo Xavier, you know that?" A faint smile tugged at her lips, and relief washed over him like a wave. She wasn't angry—not enough for this to spiral into one of their rare but intense arguments.

The past few years had been an emotional rollercoaster for Hugo. His former career in the military had shaped him, giving him purpose and identity. But the years had taken their toll. As the missions grew more demanding and recovery times longer, he'd realized it was time to leave that life behind. Turning forty had marked a painful but necessary farewell to the man he once was.

The period that followed had been like fumbling through darkness. The void left by the regimented structure of military life gnawed at him, leaving an emptiness nothing seemed to fill. Then Lita had stormed into his life like a tropical hurricane, and suddenly, everything fell into place. Her passion for life, her strength, and her warmth had given him a renewed sense of purpose.

Fate, however, had more surprises in store. When Novus was attacked and his brother Felix was nearly killed, something dormant within Hugo reawakened. The soldier inside him had come alive, hunting down the man who had pulled the trigger on his brother. Felix had survived but could no longer continue as the team leader for Novus' operations team. When Hugo was offered the position, he found the final missing piece of his puzzle—a role that blended his military expertise with civilian life. Now he had both the family he had always dreamed of and a career that fed his addiction to the adrenaline rush he'd come to crave in uniform. But it was, as always, a balancing act.

"I know," he said softly, squeezing her hand as the candlelight reflected in her eyes. "But I know I love you, and I know you love me. And we have Elektra." His voice softened even more at the mention of their daughter. "Right now, that's all that matters."

In that moment, surrounded by the gentle hum of the restaurant and the lingering bouquet of fine wine, Hugo felt both the strength and fragility of their bond. He was acutely aware of the sacrifices Lita made so he could continue his dangerous work, and his gratitude for her was greater than words could express.

8

Rome, Italy

The dark van slid silently through the shadowed streets of Via Scaliari, the driver carefully adhering to the speed limit. At this late hour, the streets were nearly deserted, save for the occasional car as they veered away from Rome's bustling center. Their destination was a safe house where they could regroup—for now, that was the only priority.

Gavrail Zaytsev sank deeper into the passenger seat, taking a few controlled breaths. It was always the same after an operation: the adrenaline that had coursed through his veins still gripped him, but as the distance from the scene of the crime grew, his pulse began to settle. A faint dizziness crept in—the familiar aftershock of tension, intoxicating and intense, no matter how many times he had been through similar missions. He held his hand up to his face and chuckled softly as he noticed the subtle trembling in his fingers. Grimacing, he let his hand fall to his lap. Inside the van's cramped interior were five men in total—himself, Marco, and three mercenaries: two Spaniards and a man from Mauritania. A motley crew of professionals, but they had carried out the mission to their employer's exact specifications, for which Gavrail was deeply grateful.

"Marco, how much farther?" His voice was hoarse after hours of silence.

Marco glanced at the expensive watch on his wrist. "Not far. Maybe five minutes. Nico, what do you think?"

The driver gave a thumbs-up without taking his eyes off the road, the van jolting over a bump. "Yeah, we should be there soon."

"Good."

Between his feet, Gavrail felt the weight of the dark backpack and the hard object inside. He pulled the case onto his lap, his fingers brushing the lock, the temptation to inspect the contents growing stronger. With careful, almost reverent hands, he opened the case and lifted the cryogenic holder into the dim light from the van's overhead lamp. A row of tiny LED lights showed the battery was nearly full.

The artificial eye rested in its transparent glass casing like a jewel in a luxury display. The design was a masterpiece of precision, every detail crafted to perfectly mimic a human eye. The synthetic whiteness of the sclera was clinically pure, almost luminous in its perfection. Around the coal-black pupil, a mesmerizing iris unfolded in shades of deep blue with subtle flecks of green—a color so natural it was hard to believe it wasn't real.

Marco let out a low laugh as he noticed Gavrail's fascinated gaze fixed on the prototype.

"Curious, I see?"

"Very," Gavrail admitted, carefully turning the holder to let the light play over its surface. "It's not every day you see something like this, is it?"

"True. But maybe it's a good idea to check in with the employer first before you get too carried away," Marco replied, his tone cautious.

Gavrail bit his lip, making a mock pistol with his hand and pointing it at Nico.

"You've always been the voice of reason, my friend."

Marco chuckled and gave him a thumbs-up in the semi-darkness.

The van turned off into the outskirts of Rome, arriving at the safe house—a seemingly abandoned building beside an old garage that had been closed for years. Wild weeds crept up the cracked sidewalks, and a scraggly,

mangy cat darted across the street like a shadow as the vehicle approached the rusty garage door.

The van rolled to a stop, and one of the men, dressed entirely in black, hopped out and quickly pulled the garage door open. The van eased into the dim space, and the door slid shut behind them with a soft metallic thud.

A single bare bulb hanging from the ceiling cast a weak, yellowish light over the garage's concrete walls. The men exited the van in hushed movements, their boots barely making a sound against the ground. Gavrail handed the backpack to Marco, who carried it carefully as they moved into the adjoining building.

The safe house was a shabby three-room apartment with a kitchen that hadn't seen life in years. Dust coated every surface, and the air carried a stale, unused scent. Marco placed the backpack gently on a small, worn table pushed against the kitchen wall. The other three men spread out, two collapsing onto a tattered sofa in the living room while the third positioned himself near the door, his gaze vigilant.

Marco turned to Gavrail with a questioning look. "So, what now?"

Gavrail pulled a cell phone from his jacket's inner pocket. "Now we call the employer and figure out how we're getting paid."

The word *paid* made Marco's eyes glint with anticipation.

Gavrail hit a speed dial and waited as the line rang twice before a metallic, distorted voice answered. The faint noises of Rome's nightlife filtered through the building's thin walls, a distant reminder of the world outside.

"Yes?"

Gavrail instinctively straightened. "The bird is in the nest. I repeat, the bird is in the nest."

There was a charged silence before the voice replied. "Excellent. Well done."

"Thank you."

"Any complications?"

"A few, but nothing we couldn't handle." Gavrail's tone was neutral, professional.

"What do you mean by 'a few'?" The metallic voice sharpened.

Suppressing a sigh, Gavrail ran a hand over his stubbled jaw. He was always irritated by clients who insisted on digging into every detail, even when the mission was accomplished. The obsessive need to micromanage, even after success, was maddening.

"They resisted," he said flatly, as though reporting the weather. "We had to shoot them."

The voice on the other end exploded. "What? I specifically ordered you to bring Dr. Rossi back alive! That was explicit! She has *Genesis,* the first prototype. I need both—*both* Dr. Rossi and Prometheus!"

Gavrail closed his eyes briefly, irritation creeping into his voice. "There was an issue. She escaped."

"Escaped?"

"Yes. She jumped out of a window and disappeared." Gavrail ran a hand through his sweat-dampened hair. "There's also another matter. The eye we recovered is in a containment unit with a battery."

The voice was silent for a few moments before responding. "Yes, I'm aware. How much charge does it have left?"

"Nearly full."

A relieved exhale came through the line. "Good. That's good. But I must have Dr. Rossi alive—she is critical. Both Prometheus and Dr. Rossi are essential."

Gavrail ground his teeth, growling low in frustration. "It wasn't our fault she escaped."

"It *was* your fault! You were tasked to follow my orders—how hard is that?"

"This means my team and I will have to stay in Rome until we find her," Gavrail said, swallowing his irritation. "This changes the plan. We won't be able to board the train to Berlin tomorrow."

"This is unacceptable!" The voice trembled with restrained fury. "You're on a deadline!"

"Dr. Rossi is injured. She can't have gotten far. We'll find her."

The silence that followed was heavy with unspoken accusations. "Find her. Then I expect you and your team to be on the train to Berlin with her and Prometheus as soon as possible."

In the dusty kitchen, the bare bulb threw long shadows across the walls as the city outside carried on, oblivious to the drama unfolding in its darkened streets. Gavrail's eyes lingered on the backpack containing the metallic holder. Time ticked relentlessly toward the deadline, and somewhere in Rome's shadowy alleys, the key to the entire mission was in hiding.

Marco let out a low chuckle, the sound echoing in the empty kitchen. "You've never been a patient man, my friend."

Inside its crystalline chamber, the artificial eye seemed to float between science and magic. The transparent casing offered an unobstructed view of every angle, as if the creators had designed it to showcase the precision of their masterpiece. Light refracted off the glass and the eye's surface, creating a play of reflections and shadows that gave life to the lifeless construct.

"It's incredible," Gavrail murmured, mesmerized by how the eye seemed to meet his gaze. It was a perfect synthesis of biology and technology, a reminder of how thin the line between natural and artificial had become. In this moment, he held the future in his hands, and deep in his mind, he knew this was the beginning of something far greater than he could comprehend.

Marco leaned in for a closer look. "Amazing how something so small can be worth so much," he said quietly, his reflection mirrored on the casing's surface.

9

Berlin, Germany

How had it come to this? Dr. Reinhart Shinkelhof bit his lip as he walked to the large window, gazing out at the rain-soaked city. He stood at the top of the west wing of the sprawling corporate complex that housed Shinkelhof Medical, one of Europe's largest pharmaceutical companies. Shinkelhof Medical had been his creation, his life's greatest pride. Over the past twenty-five years, he had taken the company from a small, insignificant enterprise to one of the leading players in the European medical market. Today, its catalog boasted an array of surgical instruments, medical devices, and pharmaceuticals—his legacy. The soft patter of rain against the glass mingled with the faint scent of fine leather that emanated from the luxurious furniture in his stately office. His hand brushed the dark-stained oak of his desk, its surface smooth under his fingertips. Everything in the room exuded success and power—the hand-knotted Persian rugs, the antique art adorning the walls, the discreet but undeniably expensive lighting. Yet it was all just a facade now. He moved toward the heavy safe hidden behind a Van Gogh painting. His fingers trembled as he turned the combination lock—right to 36, left to 24, right to 12. A muted click echoed through the room as the lock disengaged. Inside lay the quarterly report his CFO had delivered earlier that morning. He didn't even need to open it; the numbers were seared into his mind: a loss of 220 million euros in the last quarter, with the company's stock in free fall.

But what kept him awake at night was BioVita's breakthrough. Dr. Rossi's Genesis implant was revolutionary—a flawlessly functioning artificial eye powered by the body's own bioelectric field. And now, they had developed Prometheus, an even more advanced iteration. But Reinhart knew the truth: Prometheus was so cutting-edge that only Dr. Rossi's expertise could make it fully operational. Without her, it would be impossible to deploy the technology within the time frame they desperately needed. He sank into his Italian leather office chair, feeling the soft upholstery envelop him. Opening the top drawer of his desk, he pulled out a photograph. It showed him twenty-five years younger, standing proudly in front of a much smaller building, his smile radiating confidence and ambition. The young man in the photo had harbored grand dreams, and for many years, he had achieved them one by one.

But the past five years had brought change. Competitors had grown fiercer and more aggressive. New players from Asia were driving prices down. His R&D department had failed project after project, while development costs spiraled out of control. He had been forced to borrow more and more, clinging to the belief that the next breakthrough would turn everything around.

That was when the Shadow Council had approached him. A discreet meeting at an exclusive club, an offer made in careful yet unmistakable terms. They had resources, contacts, and capabilities. They could help him, but at a price—not just money, but loyalty. They would expect his services when the time came.

Now here he was, months later, deeply entangled in something he never could have imagined. When he first learned of BioVita's breakthrough, he had attempted to purchase the technology legally—Genesis, Prometheus, and Dr. Rossi's expertise. But BioVita had refused to sell. That was when he had turned to his new contacts in the Shadow Council. A researcher at BioVita had been bribed, and the information that poured in was crystal clear: all three components were essential. Genesis, the original prototype and source code. Prometheus, the advanced functionality. And Dr. Rossi herself, to integrate it all.

He had hesitated for a while, but ultimately, he had reached out to Gavrail, one of the Shadow Council's operatives.

"It needs to be a clean job," he had instructed. "We need both eye prototypes, Genesis and Prometheus, intact. And Dr. Rossi must be taken alive—without her expertise, the prototypes are worthless."

"Understood," Gavrail had replied, his voice marked by its signature cold precision. "A complete package. No compromises."

That had been then. Now was now. The rain continued to fall outside, its rhythmic drumming on the windows sounding to Reinhart like the echo of all the decisions that had led him to this moment—a point where his life's work teetered on the edge of ruin. Salvation could only come in the form of a perfectly coordinated operation, one that would secure all three keys to the future: Genesis, Prometheus, and Dr. Rossi herself.

10

Rome, Italy

An elderly woman living on the third floor had heard the muffled bangs echo through the thick stone wall. At first, she had dismissed the sounds as renovation work from a neighbor, but when desperate screams followed by more sharp bangs cut through the evening air, her trembling fingers had found their way to the phone.

"Polizia? Si, Via del Corso 247..." Her aged voice trembled. "I know this sounds strange, but something is wrong. Very wrong." She had finally convinced the skeptical operator to send a patrol. When the police arrived and understood the gravity of the situation, the area had within minutes transformed into an inferno of emergency lights and sirens that painted the old building facades in ghostly shades.

Andrea Vitti adjusted her equipment bag over her shoulder as she followed the police force into the building. Thirteen years of trauma cases on Rome's streets had hardened her, but the scene that met her still made her professional facade waver for a second. The clinically white corridor was now contaminated with dark bloodstains forming macabre patterns on the floor. The air was heavy and suffocating, a toxic mixture of gunpowder and the metallic smell of death.

"Dio mio," whispered her colleague Marco behind her.

In the first lab, three bodies lay at their workstations as if death had surprised them in the middle of an experiment. Precision instruments and test tubes were scattered across the benches, some still warm from use. What struck Andrea was the almost surgical precision in the killing - few bullet holes in walls or glass partitions, as if the killers had been experts at their craft.

A young police officer with a chalk-white face met them in the corridor. "We've searched all floors," he reported with a strained voice. "Twelve bodies in total. The entire staff... it looks like a pure execution."

Andrea nodded gravely while documenting the findings in her protocol. Minutes passed like syrup. That's when a faint sound reached her ears through the open window - an almost imperceptible scraping from the courtyard below.

"Wait!" She raised her hand to silence the others. "Did you hear that?"

The sound came again, barely audible over the sirens outside. Andrea ran toward the small courtyard, a cramped stone-paved area used for storage. Old boxes, broken office chairs, and rusty filing cabinets formed a chaotic landscape of abandoned office materials.

"Here!" she called out when she spotted a slight movement under a pile of folded boxes. "I need help here!"

Under the boxes, they found Dr. Claire Rossi, curled up in a fetal position. Her once-white lab coat was now stained with blood and dirt, her skin covered with scratches from glass shards. Her eyes were wide open but distant, filled with a horror that Andrea knew would haunt the woman for the rest of her life.

"Signora," said Andrea softly as she knelt beside Claire. Her tone was calm and steady, a professional voice trained through countless crisis situations. "Mi chiamo Andrea. We're here to help you. You're safe now."

Claire slowly turned her head toward the voice. Her lips moved but the words caught in her dry throat. Suddenly her hand shot forward and gripped Andrea's arm with a desperate strength that surprised them both.

"They... they killed everyone," she whispered hoarsely, the words broken by fear and grief. "Luca... he tried to give them what they wanted... Maria fought back... and they just... they just..." Her voice broke into a sob.

"Shh, non parlare adesso," said Andrea tenderly while carefully examining Claire's injuries. "You don't need to talk now. Let us take care of you first."

The trauma team moved like a well-oiled machine around them. Marco set up an IV drip while another colleague prepared a sedative injection. Claire trembled uncontrollably under their hands, her body in deep shock from the events.

"BP 100/70, pulse 120," reported Marco.

"Give her 5mg diazepam," instructed Andrea while securing the neck brace. "Careful now with the stretcher."

When they lifted Claire, she suddenly protested with renewed strength. "Wait! You must... you must understand..." Her voice was weak but intense. "Novus... you must contact Novus in Malmö. They took it... the prototype... the eye..." She grabbed Andrea's arm again. "Call this number." She recited the digits with surprising clarity. "Say it's from Claire Rossi. They'll kill more... so many more... if no one stops them..."

Andrea met Claire's gaze and saw something there that made her pause - a desperate look that broke through the shock and pain. She took out her phone and noted down the number, driven by an instinct she'd learned to trust over the years.

Outside, a large crowd had gathered behind the police barriers. Mobile phones and cameras flashed in the darkness as they documented the drama. Andrea pulled up the blankets to protect her patient from the curious gazes as they loaded her into the ambulance.

It was just after midnight in Rome when the phone rang at the Novus office in Malmö. The person who answered couldn't suspect that the call marked the beginning of a chain of events that would fundamentally shake both their organization and the world. In the ambulance, Andrea held Claire's hand while the city rushed by outside, and somewhere in Rome's shadowy alleys, a group of men disappeared into the night, carrying a prototype that would prove to be both worthless and invaluable at the same time.

11

Malmoe, Sweden

The clock was approaching midnight and the Novus office lay quiet and dark except for the faint light seeping out from one of the conference rooms. Hugo Xavier and Fredrika Strand sat deeply immersed in work, surrounded by computer screens and scattered piles of paper. The smell of cold coffee mingled with the scent of night rain drifting in through a half-open window.
"How was Madeleine?" Fredrika looked up from her screen, her eyes tired after hours of intense scrutiny.
Hugo leaned back in his chair and ran his hand over his stubble. "Better than expected, actually. She's furious about having to stay in the hospital, but the doctors say she needs to take it easy for a while longer."
"Typical Madeleine," Fredrika smiled. "She hates not being in control."
"Yes, and now this..." Hugo gestured toward the screens in front of them. "A traitor at Novus. It must be like poison for her."
Fredrika nodded gravely. "She built this company from the ground up. She personally approved every employee. That one of them would..." She didn't finish the sentence.
They returned to work. The sound of fingers on keyboards filled the room as they methodically went through the personnel files. Every Novus employee was scrutinized in minute detail when hired - background, finances, relationships, travels, phone calls, email correspondence - but this was the first time the Viking Protocol had been activated. The Viking Protocol was designed for precisely this type of emergency, activating a series of secret algorithms that collected snapshots from all available data sources and compiled them. The very use of the Viking Protocol stretched legal boundaries, which was partly why it had never been used. But the situation Novus faced now was entirely extraordinary, so extraordinary measures were justified.
The screen flickered.

"This is interesting," Hugo said after a while. He turned his screen toward Fredrika. "Marcus Bergman. Do you remember him?"

"The IT chief?" Fredrika furrowed her brow. "Yes, he's been here what... three years?"

"Exactly. And look at this." Hugo pointed at the screen. "His private bank account shows some strange transactions. Large sums coming in at irregular intervals from an offshore account."

Fredrika leaned closer. "When did it start?"

"About six months ago. Just before the first attack on Novus." They looked at each other. Hugo opened a new file on his computer and began typing: "Suspect #1: Marcus Bergman."

"Wait," Fredrika said suddenly. "Look at this." She turned her own screen. "Sofia Larsson from the security department. She's had several meetings outside the office with people we can't identify. And look at her movement patterns during the days before Madeleine's kidnapping."

Hugo examined the data. Sofia had been in places that coincided suspiciously well with the events. "Add her to the list," he muttered.

The hours crept by. The coffee ran out and was replaced by energy drinks. Outside the window, the city began to come to life again, but inside the conference room, they barely noticed the dawn creeping up.

"Here's something," said Fredrika, rubbing her tired eyes. "Erik Nilsson from the operations department. His sister works for a company with connections to Malaconda Villareal."

"Malaconda?" Hugo straightened up. "Are you sure?"

"Through three different shell companies, but yes, the connection is there." Fredrika started typing. "And there's more. Erik was the one who coordinated security the day Madeleine was kidnapped."

They went through the last names on the list, crossing off those they found nothing on and writing down those they had suspicions about, no matter how weak.

Hugo swore quietly. "Three suspects. All with access to sensitive information. All with the opportunity to have leaked information about our operations."

"And all people Madeleine trusted," said Fredrika in a bitter tone.

They sat quietly for a moment, letting the information sink in. Morning light began to creep through the window, casting long shadows across the walls.

"This will damage Novus," Hugo finally said. "Regardless of which one it is. Just the knowledge that we have a traitor..."

"It's already damaging the company," Fredrika interrupted. "Every day that passes without finding the guilty party is a day our reputation deteriorates. People talk. Clients get nervous."

Hugo nodded. "We need to handle this discreetly. If we confront the wrong person..."

"...we warn the guilty one," Fredrika finished his sentence.

They packed up their things as the sun rose over Malmö's skyline. Three names glowed on the screen before them: Marcus Thorn - Security Chief, Sarah Lindberg - Financial Director, and James Rodriguez - Research Director.

"What's the next step?" asked Fredrika while shutting down her computer.

Hugo looked out the window, his face hard in the morning light. "We monitor them. Around the clock. Every movement, every call, every meeting. The guilty one will make a mistake sooner or later."

"And when that happens?"

"Then we make sure Novus's reputation is restored. Permanently. But we should continue this at my place, I think. They'll start coming into the office soon."

They left the office just as the first employees began trickling in. Three innocent-looking people to be monitored. One of them a traitor. And time was running short.

12

Malmoe, Sweden

The metal key felt cold against Hugo's fingers as he inserted it into the polished lock. With a familiar motion, he turned the key and the heavy front door slid open with a dull creak. The familiar scent of home - a mixture of fresh laundry and the faint perfume Lita always wore - hit him as he stepped into the warmly lit hallway. Fredrika followed, and the sound of her steps on the parquet floor echoed faintly before she closed the door with a muffled click.

They hung up their outerwear in the hallway, where the fabric of their jackets rustled against the metal hangers. Hugo directed his steps toward the kitchen where the evening light filtered through the window, casting long shadows across the gleaming floor. Their cat, Shadow, came up to them, and Hugo bent down to pick her up with one hand while stroking her back.

"Would you like some coffee before we continue?" His voice sounded tired after the long day but professional as always. Fredrika, who had already found her way to the living room, called back with a hint of relief in her voice: "Yes, please."

In the kitchen, Hugo set Shadow down on the counter and filled the coffee maker with water, and the familiar gurgling soon began to fill the room. He pulled his phone from his pocket, and the screen lit up with a message from Lita. His eyes quickly scanned the text: I'm dropping Elektra off at mom's this morning. I have a bit of a headache so I'll come home and rest for a while. His thumbs moved quickly across the screen as he replied: Ok, I'm home. Fredrika is here and we're going through some work. Seconds ticked by before the answer came, short and with an undertone that made his gut instinct react: Ok.

The coffee aroma now filled the kitchen, rich and inviting. He poured the dark liquid into two white porcelain cups, and steam rose in small spirals toward the ceiling. With steady steps, he carried the cups to the living room where Fredrika had positioned herself at the massive oak table to the left. The laptop's bluish glow reflected in her face as she looked up. A warm smile spread across her features as she accepted the cup. "Thanks."

"No problem."

The sound of careful sips mingled with the soft clicking from the keyboard while Fredrika examined the three profiles on the screen. After a while, she leaned back in the chair, which creaked softly under the movement. A deep wrinkle formed between her eyebrows.

"I can hardly believe it. To think that one of these is a traitor. It feels completely unreal." Her voice was subdued, almost whispering.

Hugo thoughtfully ran his hand over his stubble, and the feeling of the rough strands against his fingertips was somehow calming. He took a slow sip of coffee before answering.

"It always does. Even if you think you know someone, it turns out time and time again that people always have a dark side." His tone was dark, marked by years of experience.

"Yes, of course. People are complex, I get that. But it's still a long step from having some dark sides to betraying and risking the lives of your colleagues." The frustration in her voice was palpable.

"But that's just it. There can be so many different reasons why someone would become a traitor. I mean, some of the most famous spies and traitors in history often committed their crimes for the most banal things, like excitement or money." His words echoed with the cynicism the job had taught him.

Fredrika emptied her cup with a final sip and set it down with a faint clink against the table surface. She slowly shook her head, her hair following softly with the movement.

"Yeah, I guess you're right."

Suddenly, the silence was broken by a metallic click from the front door. Hugo rose immediately, and the chair scraped against the floor. His steps were quick as he went out to the hallway. There stood Lita, noticeably pale under the warm hallway light. She moved slowly as she took off her jacket and hung it up. The faint scent of her perfume mingled with the cold air she had brought in. Hugo gave her a quick, tender kiss, noticed how cold her cheek felt against his lips.

"How are you?" His voice was soft now, completely unlike the professional tone he had used earlier with Fredrika. A worry gnawed at his stomach when he saw her pale face.

Lita shrugged with a tired movement that made her shoulders sink slightly. "I don't know, I just got a headache this morning." Her voice sounded strained as if each word cost energy.

"Did you sleep well?" He examined her face and noticed the dark circles under her eyes that he had missed earlier.

She met his gaze, and something cold, almost accusatory, flashed in her eyes. "No, not really. I had thought you would come home during the night. The last text you sent was at midnight, and you said you and Fredrika were working on something but that you'd be home soon."

The guilt hit Hugo like a punch to the gut. He felt his jaws tighten as he realized his mistake. The familiar feeling of having failed his family again crept over him. He had been so immersed in work, in hunting the traitor, that he had once again let it affect Lita. Thoughts of Elektra, their daughter, didn't make the feeling any better - he had missed yet another evening with her.

He grimaced and the wrinkles in his forehead deepened. "I'm sorry, it's completely my fault. I lost track of time." The words felt hollow as if he had said them too many times before.

She met his gaze and in the muted hallway light he saw something in her eyes that made his pulse quicken - was it distrust? Disappointment? Or something else, something worse? The silence between them became heavy, almost tangible.

"Yes, I noticed," she finally said, the words sharp as knives. "Is Fredrika here?"

Hugo swallowed, felt how dry his mouth had become. A few seconds ticked by before he nodded. "Yes, in the living room." His voice sounded foreign in his own ears.

Lita walked past him and her perfume left a faint trail in the air. Her steps were determined as she entered the living room where Fredrika immediately stood up, the chair scraping against the parquet floor. Hugo watched as Lita went forward and hugged Fredrika, a gesture that seemed both friendly and somehow marking territory.

"Hi Fredrika, how are you?" Lita's voice had changed, become warmer, more inviting. The contrast to how she had just spoken to Hugo was striking.

Fredrika smiled but Hugo could see a certain uncertainty in her posture. "I'm fine, Lita. I hope it's okay that we're sitting here working. It's just something that's difficult to work on at the office right now." The words came quickly, almost apologetically. Lita quickly shook her head and a smile played at the corners of her mouth. "It's no problem at all, Fredrika. How are you doing?" While the two women immersed themselves in small talk, Hugo instinctively felt that his presence was superfluous, perhaps even unwanted. The tense atmosphere in the room was palpable, like electricity before a thunderstorm. He quietly retreated toward the kitchen, his steps muffled against the floor. In his head, thoughts were spinning - the work of finding the traitor, Lita's suspicion, the growing divide between them. It felt like he was balancing on a knife's edge and he wasn't sure which side was more dangerous to fall toward.

The kitchen's silence enveloped him like a cold blanket when he closed the door behind him. The coffee maker was still gurgling softly, an everyday contrast to the tense atmosphere in the living room. He leaned against the kitchen counter and drew a deep sigh, feeling how the fatigue from the sleepless night began to creep into his body.

13

Malmoe, Sweden

The metal bed springs creaked softly as Madeleine Singh laboriously struggled into a sitting position at Malmö General Hospital. Every movement reminded her of the assault she had endured - the pain had transformed from the initial intense, pulsating waves to a dull, constant grinding that forced her muscles to remain in constant readiness. The unbroken tension drained her already depleted energy reserves. A deep sigh broke the silence in the room, followed by a dry smacking of her lips. With a determination that surprised even herself, she raised her voice to the empty room:
"Enough now with negative thoughts. Do something else."
The hospital room was sterile and impersonal in the way that only hospital rooms can be. Two pale watercolors in pastel colors made a halfhearted attempt to soften the white wall opposite her bed. On the other wall, modern medical technology dominated - an impressive array of monitors and medical equipment whose tubes and cables snake-like wound their way to her bed, some still connected to her body. A small flatscreen TV hung discreetly in the far corner. The pale yellow curtains that looked like they had been further bleached by countless washes framed a window where a clear blue October sky lit up the room with its bright glow.
With stiff movements, she reached for the remote and pressed the power button. The screen flickered to life and a well-dressed female reporter with perfectly styled hair and professional posture materialized on the screen. The reporter held the microphone with practiced ease while her well-styled hair swept in the light breeze.
"This is Lisa Pix from NRK News, live from Rome."
The camera swept elegantly past Lisa and zoomed in on an imposing white building across a street filled with flashing police

cars. Their rotating lights cast blue reflections against the white facade.

"What has occurred here today is completely unheard of. According to reports we've accessed, there has been some form of attack on a facility behind me. Exactly what has transpired is still unclear, but according to a source, several employees have been shot."

Lisa made a dramatic pause while bringing her hand to her earpiece. After a few tense seconds, she nodded slowly, her face serious.

"Yes, according to our source, it is now confirmed. There are at least three people dead here inside the facility called BioVita. From what we've been able to determine, it's one of the many cutting-edge medical and development companies here in Rome working on developing the very latest research findings."

Madeleine let her fingertips slowly slide across her cheek while she listened intently. The name BioVita echoed familiar in her memory but she couldn't quite place it. She turned her gaze toward the clear blue sky outside the window as if the answer was written in the thin cirrus clouds slowly drifting by.

Lisa Pix continued her report with professional intensity in her voice:

"As you can see behind me, there are at least ten police cars on site and this entire street behind me is cordoned off. I'll see if we can get hold of someone in charge who can give us more information. Follow me."

The camera followed Lisa's determined steps toward the blue and white police barriers, the tape swaying gently in the Roman breeze. Madeleine pressed her lips together while struggling with her memory. The name BioVita danced on the edge of her consciousness, teasing her with its almost-familiarity. On the TV screen, Lisa continued her hunt for information, her high heels clicking against the asphalt as she moved between the uniformed officers.

Suddenly, the memory struck Madeleine like lightning.

"Yes! That's it!"

Images from last year's conference flooded back - the cocktail party, the muted conversations, and above all, the meeting with Dr. Rossi from BioVita. They had stood in a corner of the conference hall, wine glasses in hand, discussing the latest advances in their field of research. Dr. Rossi had been an impressive woman - sharp, intelligent, and passionate when speaking about her work. It had only been a brief meeting, perhaps fifteen minutes, but Madeleine clearly remembered Dr. Rossi's intense gaze and precise formulations.

A cold feeling spread in Madeleine's stomach as she thought about Dr. Rossi, and worry grew like a dark shadow within her. She whispered into the silent room, the words heavy with concern:

"I really hope she's unharmed."

On the TV screen, Lisa Pix had given up her hunt for an interview subject. She turned to the camera with a professional smile that concealed her disappointment.

"I'll continue my search here while we return to the studio."

The image shifted abruptly to a well-dressed man in a sterile news studio. Madeleine pressed the mute button and sank back against the pillow. Minutes crept by while she stared out the window, thoughts circling around the news report and memories from the conference. The clear blue sky outside now seemed almost mockingly beautiful against the backdrop of the news from Rome.

Suddenly, a vibration from the mobile phone on the bedside table broke her thoughts. She reached for it, movements still careful to avoid the pain.

"Madeleine Singh."

The silence on the other end was almost tangible before a voice, weak and thin as paper, broke through:

"This is Dr. Rossi."

The words hung in the air like a fog of concern, and Madeleine felt her pulse quicken. The hospital room's sterile calm suddenly felt deceptive, as if the world outside its walls was holding its breath, waiting for what would come next.

"I need your help."

14

Paris, France

In the heart of Paris, where Avenue Montaigne cut through the eighth arrondissement like a sharp, elegant line of light and luxury, lay an apartment that transcended the ordinary. This wasn't just a residence – it was a manifestation of power and refinement. Malaconda Villareal, whose name was whispered with a mixture of reverence and fear in the world's most exclusive circles, had transformed this magnificent duplex into his personal empire. This October evening, a special stillness rested over the city, as if Paris itself was holding its breath in anticipation. Malaconda stood motionless by his massive panoramic window, his distinctive silhouette outlined against the Eiffel Tower's golden play of lights dancing across the violet twilight sky.

The apartment was a symphony of sophisticated luxury. Antique Persian rugs in deep wine-red and midnight blue hues spread across the hand-polished Italian marble floor like a sea of history and artistic craftsmanship. Every thread, every pattern told its own story of centuries of tradition. On the high walls hung carefully selected masterpieces – a Rothko original whose color fields pulsated with hypnotic intensity in the light from the crystal chandelier, and an early Picasso where the cubist forms seemed to move of their own accord in the shadows.

The monumental fireplace in Carrara marble spread a warm, golden glow across the room. Its flames danced in the magnificent crystal chandelier hanging from the minutely decorated stucco – a splendid relic from the Belle Époque era. The imposing bookshelves in dark-stained walnut stretched majestically from floor to ceiling, groaning under the weight of first editions and rare volumes, whose collective value exceeded what many people earned in a lifetime.

In this overwhelming environment, Malaconda sank into his favorite armchair, a handmade Chesterfield in deep cognac-colored leather from one of Italy's most prestigious tanneries. The leather creaked softly under his weight, a familiar sound reminiscent of countless hours of strategic thinking. Here, in this almost regal position, he wove his intrigues with the same precision as a spider weaves its web.

His fingers slid slowly over the exclusive leather while he mentally reviewed the latest developments. His position as leader of the Shadow Council was a paradox – simultaneously unshakeable and precarious. Unshakeable through the deep respect he still instilled in many of its members, precarious through the knowledge that several of them secretly plotted to overthrow him. The heavy scent of leather and oak mingled with the faint aroma from the open fireplace as he drew a deep breath and contemplated his situation. Perhaps this was the inevitable price for leading an organization like the Shadow Council.

His path here had been extraordinary. Before the Shadow Council, he had been an exceptionally successful businessman, amassing fortunes that would last several lifetimes. But over the years, a growing void had made itself known, an existential vacuum that neither money nor adventures could fill. It wasn't until he was invited to the legendary, secret criminal organization the Shadow Council that he finally found his true calling. There, in the shadows of established power, he had found something that could fill the void in his soul.

The transformation had been total. The most obvious change was the physical metamorphosis – a series of experimental drugs and injections had refined his body into something beyond human. As the crowning touch, he had covered his entire body with an intricate network of tattoos, whose patterns seemed to shift and move in certain lights. His final act had been to eliminate the Shadow Council's then-leader and take his place – a position he had since defended with both cunning and brutality.

Leading the Shadow Council required a strategist of exceptional caliber.

Navigating among the world's true power holders was like dancing on a knife's edge — a single misstep could mean the end. The Council's members were society's invisible architects: industry magnates, technology visionaries, financial geniuses — men and women united by an insatiable hunger for power and control.

The soft knocking on the door broke the silence like a crack in ice.

"Yes?" His voice was low but authoritative.

The door slid open noiselessly on well-oiled hinges, and a stocky, bald man in a perfectly tailored dark suit entered. His presence seemed to darken the room further.

"Leader. We have a problem." The words fell heavy in the silent air, like lead bullets in water.

15

Malmoe, Sweden

In the muted lighting of Hugo and Lita's living room, the work of analyzing the three suspected traitors continued. After almost no sleep during the night, fatigue was creeping into both Hugo and Fredrika as the clock approached lunch. The lamp's warm glow cast soft shadows on the walls while they struggled to find new clues in the seemingly endless stream of information. Fredrika pushed away the laptop with a frustrated gesture and stretched her stiff body. "God, this is tedious." Her voice was tired but determined.

Hugo let out a low chuckle. "This kind of work isn't the most fun, no."

"No, definitely not."

A sudden, loud growl from Fredrika's stomach broke the silence, and their eyes met in surprised amusement before they both burst into liberating laughter. It was as if the tension that had built up during the day released for a moment, a reminder that there was still room for joy even in dark times.

Hugo glanced at the large wall clock whose hands inexorably approached twelve. "Almost noon. I think some lunch would be appropriate. And I think Lita will wake up soon too."

Fredrika studied him with a mixture of friendly concern and caution in her gaze. "Not to pry, Hugo, but is everything okay between you two? Things felt tense earlier."

"Yeah, I suppose it is." He ran his hand through his hair with a tired gesture. "I mean, as good as it can be with the jobs we have. It's not always easy, as you know yourself."

A melancholic expression crossed Fredrika's face as she nodded slowly. The memory of her own broken engagement, torn apart by Novus's demanding work hours, was still fresh in her mind. "Yes, it's not easy. But I guess all we can do is continue as best we can."

"There's nothing else to do. And especially now with children, Elektra certainly brings much joy but it's also an extra dimension to care for."

In the kitchen, Hugo moved with practiced ease as he prepared three omelets. The eggs cracked against the bowl's edge with a distinct sound, the whisk working methodically as he added the spices. The familiar scent of melting butter filled the kitchen with its inviting aroma. Just as he had plated the finished omelets, he heard movement behind him. His trained instincts made him turn quickly.

It was Lita. Her hair was charmingly tousled and stuck out on one side like a spiky fan. A yawn escaped her, and Hugo noted with relief that the worrying pale color from earlier had disappeared from her cheeks.

With soft steps, he went forward and placed a tender kiss on her cheek. "Hi darling."

Her eyes met his, penetrating and thoughtful, before she slowly put her arms around him. "Hi yourself."

"Is the headache feeling better now?"

"A bit." Her voice was still sleepy but stronger than before.

"Good. I've made food for us. Are you hungry?"

Lita was quiet for a moment while holding his gaze captive in hers. When she spoke again, her voice was soft but intense. "I love you."

A warm wave of emotions washed through Hugo and he drew her closer, inhaling her familiar scent. "I love you too."

A radiant smile spread across her face and her pearl-white teeth gleamed in the kitchen lighting. "Good. I'll help you carry out the food."

"Thanks."

They carried out the food, glasses, and water together to the living room where Fredrika waited. She smiled warmly when she saw Lita. "Hi again. Feeling better?"

Lita placed the plates on the table with practiced ease. "Yes, much better. It was just a bit of a headache."

Lunch proceeded with light conversation, a welcome break from the day's tensions. But the peace was abruptly broken by a vibration from Hugo's phone. When he picked it up and saw Madeleine's name on the display, his gaze immediately sharpened.

"Hugo."

He listened intently. "Okay, wait Madeleine, I'm putting you on speaker." He activated the speakerphone with a quick button press. "Okay, you're on speaker with me, Lita and Fredrika." Madeleine's voice filled the room with surprising strength and clarity. "Hi Lita, hi Fredrika."

Both women instinctively leaned forward, attention sharpened. "Hi Madeleine."

"Listen, half an hour ago I got a call from Italy."

"Italy?" Hugo's voice was sharp with sudden attention.

"Yes, have you seen the news this morning?"

"No."

"Okay, it doesn't matter right now. But there's been an attack on a small medical firm down in Rome. There was a professional hit and they killed almost all employees at the company and stole their most advanced invention, an artificial, fully functional eye. But one of the employees survived, a Dr. Rossi. I've met her before and that's why she called me, she knows what Novus is and what we work with."

A heavy silence settled over the room. Hugo exchanged a long look with Fredrika, his face now hard as granite. He leaned almost imperceptibly closer to the phone. "Okay, continue."

After a tense pause, Madeleine continued: "I know this is a lot to ask now when we're busy looking for the traitor. But I promised Dr. Rossi that we'll help her get the eye back."

Hugo let his gaze wander from Fredrika to Lita and back again, weighing the options in his mind. "If we're going to do both missions, both find the traitor and retrieve Dr. Rossi's invention, we need help."

"What are you thinking, Hugo?"

"At the moment, the only others I trust besides us four are my team. If we're going to have any chance of doing this, I need to call in Mikko, Freya, and Sussie."

The black phone rested heavily on the table while they waited for Madeleine's response. When it came, it was short and decisive: "Do it."

16

Malmoe, Sweden

A few hours later, the silence was broken by a sharp knock on the door. Hugo rose slowly from the worn leather armchair while the afternoon light filtered through the half-drawn curtains. His steps echoed dully against the parquet floor as he walked through the dimly lit hallway. When he opened the door, he was met by two familiar faces.

Freya, tall and athletic with her raven-black hair neatly tied in a tight ponytail, was first across the threshold. Her movements were smooth and controlled, typical for someone with her specialized training. She gave Hugo a quick but warm hug, and the scent of her characteristic jasmine perfume mingled with the cold autumn air.

"Hi Hugo, all well?" Her dark eyes examined him attentively, as if searching for signs of concern.

"Hi Freya, everything's fine. Or as fine as it can be." His voice was steady but with an undertone of fatigue that didn't escape her trained ear.

Close behind came Sussie Andersen, shorter in stature with sand-colored hair falling in soft waves over her shoulders. When she hugged Hugo, her embrace felt soothing, like a reminder of older times when the situation had been less complicated.

"Hugo, good to see you." Her voice was soft but determined.

Hugo's arms closed around her in a protective gesture. "Sussie, I'm glad you're here." His words were sincere, weighted by recent events.

With practiced movements, Hugo took their jackets - Freya's black leather jacket and Sussie's navy coat - and hung them up carefully. He nodded toward the living room where warm lamps spread a welcoming glow. "Lita and Fredrika are in there. Would you like coffee?"

Both women nodded simultaneously, a synchronization that came from years of collaboration. "Yes, please."

While Hugo disappeared into the kitchen, where the coffee machine hummed familiarly, he heard the muffled murmur of women's voices from the living room. The conversation flowed naturally, as if they were trying to hold onto a piece of normality in a situation that was anything but normal. He returned with two steaming cups of dark roasted coffee, the steam rising like thin spirals in the air.

Sussie gratefully accepted her cup and let it warm her hands while she carefully tasted the hot beverage. "Thanks."

Lita, sitting on the sofa with her legs tucked under her, let out a low laugh that didn't quite reach her eyes. "This is almost quite a gathering here. I hadn't expected that when I woke up this morning."

Fredrika shook her head, her face was tense but she forced out a strained smile. "No, neither did I. But you should know that I'm very grateful we can be here."

"That's not how I meant it," Lita hurried to say while meeting Hugo's gaze with warmth in her eyes. "Of course you're welcome here as much as you want."

They sank into the sofa group, and despite the tense atmosphere, the conversation felt almost natural. The scent of freshly brewed coffee filled the room and for a brief moment, one could almost forget the gravity of the situation.

After about fifteen minutes, the stillness was broken by another knock on the door, stronger this time. Hugo rose again and went out to the hall. When he opened it, he was met by an imposing figure that made the doorframe seem undersized. Mikko Solemainen, with his bushy, fair hair and massive build, was an impressive sight. His bear hug almost lifted Hugo from the floor, and the scent of leather and outdoor air followed him in.

"Hugo!" Mikko's voice thundered through the hall.

Hugo struggled to keep air in his lungs under the powerful embrace. "Mikko, good to see you."

When Mikko finally let go, his booming laughter echoed between the walls. "What's happening? Is everything okay? Why aren't we meeting down at headquarters?"

Hugo took care of Mikko's weather-beaten leather jacket while gesturing toward the living room. "The others are in there. I'll get you a cup of coffee."

Mikko's broad smile lit up his face as he stepped into the living room. His surprised exclamation made the walls vibrate. "Oh, there's quite a collection of strong women here!"

Hugo smiled to himself while preparing another cup of coffee. When he returned to the living room, Mikko had already got everyone laughing at something. The big man gratefully accepted the cup. "Thanks, my friend."

The mood stayed relaxed for a few more minutes before Hugo felt it was time. He straightened up, and the sound of his throat-clearing drew everyone's attention to him. The room immediately fell silent, and the light atmosphere was replaced by focused expectation.

"Listen," he began, his voice now deeper and more serious, "even though this is as pleasant as it can be, there's something behind all this. We're in the middle of a unique situation here that we've never been in before. And that's why we've called you in."

Freya, whose body now radiated tense attention, sat on the edge of the sofa like a coiled spring. "I assume it has something to do with Madeleine, right? It's been about a week that she's been in the hospital already. What's happened?"

Hugo took a deep breath, feelings of worry and determination battled within him as he began to tell. His voice was steady as he recounted the conversation with Madeleine and their latest mission. When he described the task of finding the traitor within Novus, the temperature in the room dropped noticeably.

Fredrika took over the story about the company in Rome, her voice charged with suppressed concern as she described the attack.

Sussie thoughtfully stroked her cheek with her finger, her technically trained brain already in full swing analyzing the situation. "Sounds like this could develop into a busy week for us if this little meeting is what I think it is."

Hugo let his gaze slowly slide over his assembled colleagues - Freya with her deadly precision, Sussie and her technical brilliance, and Mikko with his indomitable strength. His voice was low but intense when he spoke. "Listen, this depends on us. We're under pressure in a way we haven't been before. Both a possible traitor and now also a mission. And Madeleine wants us to solve both."

Mikko clenched his massive fist and slammed it into his knee with a force that made the sofa shake. His face was hard with determination when he answered. "You know you can trust us. We'll do everything we can."

17

Berlin, Germany

Dr. Reinhart Shinkelhof sat in the private sauna, feeling the intense heat envelop his aging body. The scent of cedar wood and heated pine filled his senses while beads of sweat slowly ran down his forehead. Taking a sauna had always been his refuge, a place for contemplation, and over the years, this ritual had become increasingly important. Now, at the height of his career as CEO of Shinkelhof Medical, he had built this private oasis directly connected to his office - a luxury that reminded him of his position, even if it was currently threatened.

His thoughts swirled like restless birds while he tried to find some form of peace of mind. The past year had been a nightmare of proportions he had never experienced before. Crises had followed one another in a merciless chain reaction that he, despite his long experience in corporate management, had failed to break. Like dominoes, the setbacks had fallen, one after another, transforming Shinkelhof Medical from a respected, profitable company to one that was now bleeding money. In sheer desperation, he had done the unthinkable - promised the market the impossible: an artificial eye that could restore sight to millions of blind people. A promise that now felt like a noose around his neck.

Sweat ran in streams while he took deep, controlled breaths. The heat burned like fire against his skin, but it still seemed unable to burn away the gnawing worry that had been his constant companion for the past year. The only bright spot, if one could call it that, was the offer of a place in the Shadow Council. In his desperation, he had accepted without hesitation, convinced he could utilize the council's extensive resources to steal a competitor's technology and thereby save his own failed project.

With a steady hand, he reached for the copper-shimmering ladle that lay in the antique water bowl. The water glittered in the muted light as he poured it over the glowing sauna heaters. A hissing cloud of steam rose up and enveloped him in a suffocating heat that made his skin tingle.

Suddenly, the stillness was broken by a knock on the door. He startled, his nerves on edge. Through the steamy glass window, he glimpsed a slim hand that quickly withdrew.

"Sir? It's Janice." His secretary's voice was muffled through the door.

Reinhart straightened up and pulled the damp towel tighter around himself. "Yes?"

"You have a phone call."

"Tell them I'll call back." His voice sounded irritated, even to his own ears.

"I tried telling the man on the phone that, but he says it's urgent." There was a note of concern in her voice that made him sharpen his attention.

"Urgent?" His heart began beating faster.

"He said I should say seven hills. I don't know what he meant by that but I promised to relay it to you."

Reinhart felt his blood turn to ice in his veins. He froze, while the code word echoed in his head. "Okay, I'm coming. Give me a minute."

"Okay." Janice's steps quickly disappeared from the door.

With trembling hands, he hurried out of the sauna, dried himself hastily, and wrapped the Egyptian cotton robe around himself. When he stormed out through the door, he almost collided with Janice who was waiting with the phone.

"Thank you." He grabbed the phone while trying to control his breathlessness. Seven hills - the code word that he and Gavrail had agreed upon for the operation against BioVita - made his pulse race.

"Reinhart." His voice was tense when he answered the phone, still breathless from the sauna.

A raspy voice answered. "News from Rome. The police have found a survivor in BioVita's courtyard. Dr. Rossi. She's in a hospital in Rome now."

Reinhart's face contorted with rage and he clenched his fist so hard his knuckles whitened. The sweat from the sauna suddenly felt cold against his skin. "What the hell are you saying?"

"Dr. Rossi survived. She hid in the courtyard and..."

"I heard what you said!" Reinhart roared. Janice, who was still nearby, jumped at his sudden outburst. With a quick gesture, he waved her away. "Keep me updated," he hissed and ended the call.

With trembling fingers, he immediately dialed Gavrail's number. After two rings, a hoarse voice answered.

"Yes?"

"You incompetent bastard!" Reinhart could barely control his rage. "The police have her!"

"Quiet! Don't use..."

"Shut up!" Reinhart began pacing back and forth in the room, the robe fluttering around him. "Dr. Rossi is in a hospital in Rome. The police have her. Do you know what that means?"

A long silence followed. "Explain."

"There's no possibility of you kidnapping her now, is there! I need her!" Reinhart ran his hand through his damp hair in frustration. "Damn you, Gavrail. You've ruined everything!"

"Now that the police have her, it will be almost impossible to..."

"Almost is not the same as impossible." Gavrail interrupted him. "We'll fix this."

"How? She's under police guard at a hospital!"

"It doesn't matter. We have people here. Contacts. We'll handle this." Gavrail's tone was cold and professional. "But it will cost extra."

Reinhart closed his eyes and massaged his temples. More money, more risk. But what choice did he have?

"Do what's necessary," he finally said. "But Gavrail... fail again and the consequences will be... serious."

A low laugh echoed in the receiver. "Don't threaten me, Reinhart. You have no idea who you're dealing with." The call ended abruptly.

Reinhart stared at the silent phone while panic grew within him. He had bet everything on this, and now his entire future balanced on a knife's edge. In a fit of frustration, he threw the phone across the room. It hit the wall with a satisfying crash and fell to the floor in pieces.

The sauna's warmth had now completely left his body, replaced by an icy feeling of horror. Somewhere in Rome, the key to his survival lay in a hospital, guarded by police, while time inexorably ticked toward his deadline with the Shadow Council.

18

Malmoe, Sweden

Her beautiful eyes were like deep wells of warmth and love, something Hugo never tired of losing himself in. Lita drew him closer, and he felt the warmth from her body flow through his own. They stood together in their bedroom, embraced in the muted light from the bedside lamp. Through the closed door to the hall, the others' voices penetrated, especially Mikko's characteristic bass voice that rolled like thunder through the walls.

Hugo tenderly brushed away a rebellious coal-black lock that had fallen over Lita's forehead. His fingers lingered on her cheek. "You're the best I know, darling. You know that." His voice was soft, almost whispering.

Lita lifted her gaze to him, and an impish smile spread across her lips. "Hugo Xavier, you know exactly all the right words a woman wants to hear."

Hugo chuckled softly and bent down to kiss her. Her lips were soft, with an enchanting taste of vanilla and tropical fruit from her lip gloss.

"When this is over, I promise we'll take a long vacation, just you, me, and Elektra." His words were a promise, a future dream to hold onto.

"Somewhere warm?" Hope sparkled in her eyes.

"Of course, Greece maybe?"

Lita's eyes lit up like stars. "Yes, one of the Greek islands. We can go boating, eat good food and lie by the pool and just relax."

He kissed her again, deeper this time, as if to seal the promise. "Good, it's a deal."

Lita nodded toward the door, her face becoming more serious. "So you and Sussie are going down to Rome to try to help down there?"

"Yes, and Freya, Mikko, and Fredrika will continue working on hunting the traitor."

A worried wrinkle appeared between Lita's eyebrows. "Is it smart to split up?"

"For now we have no choice. If we're going to complete both missions, we have to split up. And considering how few we are at the moment, this is the best solution." His voice was steady, professional, but with an undertone of apology.

Lita laid her head against his chest, and he could feel her heartbeat against his own. "I understand. Just make sure you come back in one piece."

He pulled her closer, buried his nose in her hair that smelled of jasmine. "I promise."

When they returned to the living room, Hugo let his gaze slowly sweep over the group. "So, everyone knows what they're doing? No one has any doubts about this?"

Freya, Sussie, Fredrika, Mikko, and Hugo exchanged glances while Lita remained in the doorframe as a silent observer.

Despite the gravity of the situation, Hugo felt a wave of confidence wash over him. His team - Freya with her deadly precision, Sussie with her technical genius, and Mikko with his indomitable strength - were more than just colleagues. They had stared death in the face together, and such experiences created bonds that went deeper than ordinary friendship, bonds that were forged in fire and trials.

Mikko's booming laugh made the window panes vibrate. "You know that Hugo, we'll follow you anywhere. After everything we've been through, you know that."

Hugo looked at his team and felt warmth spread in his chest, a mixture of pride and gratitude.

The farewell was brief but emotional. He and Sussie retrieved their packed bags with equipment and clothes from the hall and went down to the waiting taxi. As the car began rolling toward Kastrup, Hugo looked up at the apartment window where Lita's silhouette was outlined against the warm light from inside.

Sussie, sitting beside him in the back seat, followed his gaze. "She loves you, you know." Her voice was soft, almost sisterly.

Hugo smiled, without taking his eyes from the window. "Yes, I know."

"You should count yourself lucky with what you have, Hugo."
"I do, every day." His voice was filled with conviction.
The taxi glided over the Öresund Bridge, its tires singing against the asphalt, before dropping them off at Kastrup. Security was passed routinely, and an hour later they sank into their airplane seats heading for Rome.
Hugo looked thoughtfully out the window at the green lawns that bordered the runway. When the plane took off, the landscape disappeared beneath them, and for a moment he was alone with his thoughts in the rising metal tube, while Denmark shrank to a patchwork of green and blue beneath them.

19

Malmoe, Sweden

Freya stood by the large living room window, looking out over Magistratsparken while the evening sun painted the sky in muted orange tones. She held a cup of coffee in her hand, her third for the day, and breathed in the strong aroma. Behind her, Mikko sat on the sofa with a notepad in front of him where he had written down the three names that were their main suspects: Marcus Thorn - Security Chief, Sarah Lindberg - Financial Director, and James Rodriguez - Research Director. Fredrika sat in the armchair opposite with her legs tucked under her, her laptop open in her lap where she was going through the personnel files. "It still feels unreal that one of these three would be a traitor," she mumbled while her fingers danced over the keyboard. "I've worked with all of them for several years."

"That's exactly why we must be extra careful," said Freya, turning from the window. "We can't let personal relationships cloud our judgment."

Mikko stretched his massive body and the sofa creaked under his weight. "But how do we do this without raising suspicions? If one of them really is a traitor, they'll be on guard."

Lita, who had just come in from the kitchen with a fresh pot of coffee, paused. "Why not use that security audit planned for next month? You could move it forward and call all three in for individual reviews."

Freya turned quickly toward her. "The security audit? The one that was planned for the quarterly review?"

"Exactly, Hugo mentioned it earlier," Lita nodded. "No one would question why you're calling them in for that. It's routine, after all."

"Lita, you're a genius," exclaimed Fredrika and immediately began typing on her computer. "I can send out the summons right now. Given their positions, none of them can refuse to participate."

Mikko leaned forward, his eyes intense. "And during the interviews we can test them, see how they react to certain questions without revealing our real purpose."

Freya set down her coffee cup and began pacing the room. "We have to be strategic. Who do we start with?"

"Marcus Thorn," said Fredrika decisively. "As Security Chief, he'll expect to be first, and it would raise suspicions if we didn't start with him."

Over the following hours, they refined their strategy. Fredrika formulated emails that sounded completely routine yet demanded immediate attendance. Freya and Mikko developed an interview technique that would let them evaluate each suspect's reactions without revealing their true agenda.

By nearly nine in the evening, everything was prepared. The emails had been sent and all three suspects had confirmed they would appear at Novus headquarters the following morning.

"Then it's time," said Freya, standing up. She checked her phone one last time. "We'll meet at the office at seven tomorrow. I want to go through everything one final time before Marcus arrives at nine."

They gathered their things and put on their jackets in the hall. Lita stood leaning against the doorframe, watching them.

"Be careful," she said softly. "One of them has already been involved in an attack. We don't know what they're capable of."

Freya hugged her quickly. "We're always careful. And thanks for letting us be here."

They took the elevator down and walked out into the cool evening air. Mikko's large SUV was parked by the curb, its black paint reflecting the glow of the street lamps. They got in the car, Mikko behind the wheel, Freya in the passenger seat, and Fredrika in the back seat with her laptop still open.

During the drive down to Novus headquarters, they went through the plan one last time. The streets were almost empty at this time, and the building rose like a dark silhouette against the night sky as they turned into the parking lot.

They went around to the back and Fredrika swiped a keycard over a card reader at a thick metal door. The door clicked and opened. They went in and down to a few rooms in the basement where several beds and sofas were lined up. Freya and Fredrika went into one room while Mikko took another.

"See you tomorrow. Sleep well."

At 8:55 the next morning, they sat in the conference room on the third floor. Freya stood by the window looking down at street level where Marcus Thorn's black BMW was just turning into the parking lot. She turned to the others.

"He's here."

Mikko positioned himself strategically at the far end of the room, his impressive physique a silent but effective means of pressure. Fredrika opened her laptop and started the recording program. Freya took a seat at the head of the table, perfectly positioned to read Marcus's body language.

At exactly nine o'clock, there was a knock on the door and Marcus Thorn stepped in. He was a well-built man in his forties, dressed in a perfectly tailored dark blue suit. His posture was relaxed but alert, typical for someone with his background in security.

"Good morning," he said with a professional smile. "Security audit already? I thought that was planned for next month. I know things have been a bit chaotic lately, but still."

Freya smiled back, an exercise in controlled friendliness. "We had reason to move it forward. Thank you for coming on such short notice."

Marcus sat down, his movements controlled and precise. "Of course. As Security Chief, I must set a good example."

Freya opened a thin folder in front of her. "Let's start with the routine questions. Have you noticed any deviations in security protocols during the last three months? Apart from what happened with Madeleine, of course."

Marcus leaned back in his chair, his eyes focused on Freya. "Of course during the last mission where we were attacked again. Despite all our measures and improvements, we were attacked and even Madeleine was kidnapped. But before that, there were no major deviations. We had a couple of minor incidents with incorrectly programmed keycards in February, but that was resolved within 24 hours."

Freya noted how his right hand rested relaxed on the table, while his left lay in his lap, out of sight. A classic defensive technique she recognized from interrogation training.

"And regarding information security? Particularly concerning Project Azure?"

For a fraction of a second, Marcus's jaw muscles tensed before he answered. "All protocols were followed to the letter. I personally oversaw security around that project."

Mikko cleared his throat slightly from his position, and Marcus cast a quick glance in his direction before returning his focus to Freya.

"Can you describe exactly what security measures were implemented for Project Azure?" Freya kept her voice neutral while observing every micro-expression in Marcus's face.

"Of course." Marcus began counting off the measures on his fingers. "Separate servers with triple encryption, biometric access for all entrances to the lab, logging of all data traffic, and weekly security reviews with the project team."

Fredrika typed silently on her laptop while Freya continued.

"And you personally oversaw all these aspects?"

"Yes, that's correct." Marcus's voice was steady, but Freya noticed his breathing had become slightly faster.

"Interesting," said Freya and pulled out a document from the folder. "Because according to this report, you were on vacation in Dubai during the second week of February, right when the critical tests for Project Azure were conducted. How could you personally oversee security then?"

An almost imperceptible movement shot through Marcus's body, like an electric shock. His smile disappeared for a millisecond before returning, but now with a harder edge.

"Ah, I should have been clearer," he said, his voice still controlled but with an almost imperceptible tremor. "I naturally delegated the monitoring to my deputy, Jens, during my absence, but I received daily reports and could remotely control all critical systems from my secure laptop."

Freya leaned forward, her eyes locked on his. "And these daily reports, are they documented in the system?"

"Of course," Marcus replied quickly, perhaps a bit too quickly. "I can retrieve them for you after the meeting."

"That would be very helpful," said Freya with a small smile. "We'll surely have more questions once we've gone through them."

20

Rome, Italy

Hugo drank the last of his coffee and slowly set the antique porcelain cup down on the white linen tablecloth. The grand hotel dining room, with its crystal chandeliers and Renaissance ceiling frescoes, was half-filled with guests moving between the breakfast buffet like a sleepy stream of people. Morning light filtered through the tall windows, casting shadowy patterns on the marble floor.

He and Sussie had landed just after midnight at Fiumicino, Rome's largest airport. The late hour had rendered the usually chaotic airport unusually calm, and the baggage carousel delivered their suitcases in an almost eerie stillness. Fredrika's contact, Luigi Valetta, had met them at the arrivals hall and driven them through Rome's night-shrouded streets to this elegant hotel near the hospital where Dr. Rossi was staying.

A soft voice interrupted his thoughts. "Is everything all right?" He looked up to meet the gaze of a young waitress in a crisp white blouse and an elegant black skirt. Her words carried a musical tone, colored by her accent.

"Yes, thank you. Everything is just perfect. Very delicious," he said, lifting the cup in an appreciative gesture.

Her smile brightened her entire face. "Excellent."

A few minutes later, Sussie appeared in the dining room. Her blonde hair was neatly tied back in a ponytail that swayed as she walked. The deep red jacket she wore contrasted elegantly with her black trousers, and on her back was the same discreet black backpack as the one by Hugo's feet. She headed straight for the coffee machine before joining him at the table.

Hugo couldn't help but smile at her tired expression. "Sleep well?"

She took a deep sip of her coffee and shook her head. "Not really. All the pillows are too hard. I mean, what are the odds?

When there are eight pillows, you'd think at least one would be soft enough."

He chuckled softly. His ability to fall asleep was almost legendary within the team—no matter the place or circumstances, he could drift off within minutes. Over the years, he'd grown to appreciate this gift more and more.

"You're right. I completely agree," he teased lightly.

She glared at him over the rim of her coffee cup. "But you look like you slept well."

"I did, like a log."

Sussie rolled her eyes but couldn't hide a small smile. "I'm jealous, Hugo. Truly."

"Grab something to eat—it'll help."

"You're right."

She soon returned with a plate full of fresh bread, cheese, and fruit. After finishing her meal, she leaned back, looking much more content.

"Better?" Hugo asked.

She gave him a thumbs-up. "Much. Luigi was picking us up at eight, right?"

"Yes. In ten minutes."

The plan was well-organized, thanks to Fredrika's connections. Navigating Rome's morning traffic was a challenge few foreigners dared tackle, but Luigi was an experienced guide through the city's chaotic street network.

Right at eight o'clock, Luigi appeared at the dining room entrance, his dark hair neatly combed and his suit impeccable. Sussie noticed his arrival. "Hugo, Luigi is here."

"Good. Let's get going."

They met Luigi at the entrance, and his face lit up with a warm smile. "Buongiorno. Is everything all right? Did you have a pleasant night?"

"Absolutely. It's a very fine hotel," Hugo replied.

Luigi's smile widened. "Excellent. I've been instructed to get you swiftly to the hospital where Dr. Rossi is. So, if you're ready, I recommend we head out. Morning traffic in Rome can be... challenging."

During the drive through Rome, Luigi turned into an enthusiastic guide, his voice brimming with passion as he pointed out historical landmarks and shared fascinating anecdotes. The thirty-minute journey felt like a private tour of the Eternal City. When they reached the hospital, Luigi eased the car to a stop.
"Here we are. I hope the ride was to your satisfaction?"
Hugo gave him a warm smile and placed a hand on Luigi's arm. "The best taxi ride I've had in Rome—actually, the best in all of Europe."
Inside the hospital's sterile walls, Luigi led them to the reception desk, where he exchanged a quick conversation in Italian. His thumbs-up signaled success. "Dr. Rossi is on the fifth floor, under police protection. I'll take you up there; apparently, someone else will meet you after that. I'm not allowed to go further."
On the fifth floor, they were met by a plainclothes police officer whose watchful eyes scrutinized them carefully before he nodded. "Follow me."
Luigi stayed behind with an encouraging smile. "I'll wait here."
The hallway seemed endless as they followed the officer to Dr. Rossi's room. Inside, they were met with a sight that made Hugo pause. A woman lay in the bed, wrapped in bandages and surrounded by beeping machines and humming monitors. The tubes and wires tethering her to the equipment formed a complex web of life and technology.
The policeman approached the bed. "Dr. Rossi? They're here."
When Dr. Rossi opened her eyes, they burned with an intensity that surprised Hugo. Despite the bandages and visible injuries, she radiated an indomitable strength.
"Come closer," her voice was hoarse but firm.
Hugo and Sussie stepped closer to the bed. "My name is Hugo Xavier, and this is Sussie Mortensen. We're from Novus."
Dr. Rossi's one visible eye flared with a feverish intensity that had nothing to do with her injuries, though it subsided after a moment. When she spoke, her voice was filled with a mix of anger and triumph.

"I know who tried to kill me—and who murdered everyone at my company."

21

Novus HQ, Malmoe, Sweden

The evening light seeped through the tall glass walls of Fredrika's office on the second floor of Novus' headquarters. The sun's rays reflected off Malmö's dark harbor waters, casting a golden glow over the minimalist room with its sleek metal furniture and high-tech equipment. The cool air from the ventilation system carried a faint aroma of freshly brewed coffee from the break room next door.

Fredrika sat upright at her matte black desk while Freya stood by the window, her poised stance revealing years of military training. In the corner, Mikko occupied nearly the entire gray sofa with his massive frame—a testament to two decades as an elite soldier. Three beige folders lay spread out on the desk like puzzle pieces in a larger mystery.

"Okay," Fredrika said with a voice that commanded authority, opening her high-performance laptop with a decisive motion. "Let's go through what we have." Her fingers moved quickly over the keyboard, and three detailed timelines were projected onto the clear glass wall. "Sarah Lindberg first."

Freya turned from the window, her steps silent against the polished wood floor. "She seemed genuinely surprised during most of the interview. I didn't observe any microexpressions that indicated deceit."

Mikko adjusted his rumpled blazer as he flipped through his neatly organized notes. His deep voice echoed faintly in the room. "Her alibi is airtight, like a submarine hatch. The strategy meeting in Stockholm with Ericsson had hundreds of witnesses and video documentation. No way she could have been in two places at once."

"Also," Fredrika interjected while scrolling rapidly through multiple data screens, "her finances are pristine. Every single krona is traceable—legitimate sources like her salary and some impressive tech investments."

Freya moved with feline grace to Fredrika's desk, picking up Marcus Thorn's folder. The dry rustle of paper accompanied her movement. "But these two..." She placed the folder next to James Rodriguez's file with a heavy thud. "Something doesn't add up here."

"Marcus sweated like a pig during the interview," Mikko said, rising from the sofa with a groan of protest from the springs. His shadow fell across the floor like a dark curtain. "That story about Dubai... it was as fake as a three-kilo banknote. I could practically smell the lies."

Fredrika turned her high-resolution screen toward her colleagues with a sharp motion. The blue light from the display reflected off her glasses.

"His explanation about remote monitoring is a house of cards ready to collapse. The logs are crystal clear—no external access was recorded during the critical period. Not a single digital footprint."

"James was just as suspicious," Freya pointed out, nervously drumming her fingers on the edge of the table. "His answers about the research data were like fog—the closer you got, the more they dissolved. And his explanation for late-night lab visits the week before the breach..." She shook her head, her long dark hair falling like a curtain over her shoulders.

A heavy silence settled over the room, broken only by the faint hum of the ventilation system and the distant murmur of traffic far below. The evening sun cast fiery streaks through the windows, transforming Malmö's skyline into a burning horizon of copper and gold. The air felt electric, charged with unspoken suspicions.

Suddenly, Mikko straightened his massive frame, and the sofa springs groaned in protest. "We need to isolate them. Get them out of their comfort zones. Apply pressure until someone cracks." His voice was low but intense, like distant thunder.

Freya turned to him, her eyes narrowing thoughtfully. "Go on."

"Turning Torso," Fredrika interjected before Mikko could respond. Her voice sliced through the air like a laser. "We have a secure floor there, the one Madeleine used for her more... discreet meetings."

"Perfect," Freya nodded, a predatory smile tugging at the corners of her lips. "We'll bring them there under the pretense of continued security interviews. Keep them separated but close enough to sense each other's presence. Let paranoia do half the work."

Fredrika's fingers flew across the keyboard with military precision. "The floor can be ready within sixty minutes. But the transport needs to be seamless. No witnesses, no questions."

Mikko smiled—a gesture that on his rugged face looked more like a warning than a welcome. "I'll take Marcus in my car. My... physical presence tends to have a calming effect on nervous souls."

"James is mine," Freya said with a tone of controlled intensity. "We'll stick with the standard explanation—neutral setting for further security interviews. Routine." Her smile was devoid of warmth. "Most people will swallow anything if it's served with the right garnish of bureaucracy."

Thirty tense minutes later, two vehicles slid out of Novus' underground parking garage like silent predators on the hunt. Leading the convoy was a matte black SUV, with Mikko dominating the driver's seat, his massive frame exuding an air of authority, while Marcus Thorn sat hunched in the passenger seat, his nervous fingers unconsciously fiddling with his shirt buttons. In the rearview mirror, Mikko could see Freya's silver-gray sedan gliding like a shadow behind them, James Rodriguez visible through the tinted windshield.

Fredrika had stayed behind to continue working on the case and provide updates to Madeleine. Every breath, every micro-expression would be scrutinized. No detail would escape their analysis.

Ten minutes later, the descending sun turned Turning Torso's twisting form into a spiral of liquid gold against the violet evening sky. The building loomed like a titanic corkscrew over Malmö's skyline, its glass façade reflecting the last rays of sunlight in a hypnotic dance of light and shadow. The low rumble of tires on concrete echoed through the underground garage as the vehicles slid into their reserved spots.

The private elevator, clad in brushed steel and bathed in dim lighting, hummed softly as it carried them upward. The subtle change in air pressure made their ears pop—a gentle reminder of their swift ascent toward the skyscraper's upper floors. James Rodriguez tried to mask his nervousness with an air of professional curiosity.

"Impressive view," he remarked, his voice almost steady but with a faint tremor as they stepped out of the elevator. Below, Malmö stretched out like an electronic circuit board of twinkling lights, while the Öresund Bridge arched like a luminous ribbon toward Denmark in the distance.

"This is one of our security-certified facilities," Freya explained, her tone perfectly balanced between professional and disarming as she guided them down a corridor lined with soundproof materials. Her footsteps were barely audible against the matte black floor. "Here, we can continue our discussions without... distractions."

Mikko opened a door to the left with a motion that seemed improbably graceful for his size. "Mr. Thorn," he said, his voice smooth as velvet over steel, "please step inside." It wasn't a request, though the words were phrased as one.

On the opposite side of the corridor, Freya led James to an identical room. "Dr. Rodriguez, please step in." Her smile didn't reach her eyes.

When the doors closed with soft clicks, Freya and Mikko exchanged a long look in the corridor's play of shadows. The words that followed were little more than whispers, but they carried an unmistakable weight of resolve.

"Fredrika will be here in ten with the equipment," Freya breathed. "Then we start pulling threads. One at a time, until the whole fabric unravels."

Mikko nodded gravely, his massive shadow cast like a dark omen against the wall. "This time, we'll uncover the truth," he rumbled. "No matter how deeply it's buried."

22

Malmoe, Sweden

Inside the apartment, they were greeted by two men in tailored black suits—Jonas Kvist and Peter Rydell from Novus' security team. Their presence filled the subtly lit corridor with an air of palpable professionalism, making the atmosphere vibrate with tense anticipation. They exchanged barely perceptible nods with Mikko and Freya before seamlessly taking over responsibility for the suspects.

"This way, Mr. Thorn," said Jonas, his voice smooth as velvet but with an underlying steel core. His hand rested on Marcus's shoulder with a grip that was polite yet uncompromising as he directed him toward the interrogation room on the right. The expensive cologne emanating from Marcus's suit mingled with the antiseptic scent permeating the corridor.

Peter escorted James with the same silent efficiency, his footsteps inaudible against the polished marble floor. The interrogation rooms, identically furnished with brushed steel tables and ergonomic black leather chairs, were dominated by a wall of panoramic windows. Beyond the reinforced glass, the Öresund stretched out like a black ribbon of silk, with Denmark's coastline glimmering faintly in the distance, a string of scattered diamonds against the velvety night sky.

Twenty minutes later, Freya's determined heels echoed down the corridor as she arrived carrying a silver Halliburton case. The faint hum of the air conditioning was interrupted by her quick breaths as she entered the smaller control room between the interrogation rooms, where Fredrika had already set up a high-tech command center. High-definition monitors covered the walls, bathing the room in a cold, blue glow. Each displayed crystal-clear footage from the interrogation rooms alongside pulsing graphs of real-time data.

"Quantum Bio-Response Analyzer," Freya explained as her fingers expertly unlocked the case with surgical precision. The muted click of the latches echoed as she began connecting the thin, snake-like cables to the advanced system in the control room. "Next-generation lie detector. It captures everything from microscopic facial twitches to the smallest variations in vocal overtones." The system hummed to life with a low, resonant sound, as though the air itself vibrated with its hidden power.

"Connection complete," Fredrika confirmed after several minutes of focused silence. "We have full sensor and video monitoring from both rooms." Her voice carried an undertone of satisfaction at the flawless technical setup.

Mikko stood motionless by the door, his presence as commanding as gravity itself in his jet-black suit. "We'll start with James. He's the weakest link." His words were heavy, pressing against the compressed air of the room.

The three of them moved like a well-oiled machine into the left interrogation room, where James sat hunched at the steel table. His fingers tapped out a nervous rhythm against the cold metal surface, the sound unnervingly sharp in the sterile quiet. Beads of sweat already glistened on his forehead under the fluorescent lights, and the scent of his fear seemed almost tangible in the sterile air.

Fredrika slid gracefully into the chair opposite him, feline in her movements, while Freya and Mikko positioned themselves in shadowy corners of the room, silent sentinels amplifying the claustrophobic sense of confinement. The faint hum of the ventilation system was the only sound breaking the tense silence.

"Dr. Rodriguez," Fredrika began, her voice precise and sharp as a scalpel. "Let's talk about the night of September 15." Her words fell like icy drops into the room.

In the control room, the sensors' graphs spiked wildly as James's stress levels soared. His pupils dilated noticeably, black voids in his pale face, and another wave of micro-sweat broke out on his brow, shimmering under the harsh light.

"I... I was home," James stammered, his voice trembling like a leaf in the wind.

"Lie," Freya whispered sharply into her discreet earpiece, her eyes locked on the chaotic sensor data streaming in from the adjacent room. "Extreme deviation in vocal patterns. His vocal cords are vibrating at the wrong frequency."

"Fascinating," Fredrika replied, her tone as calm as a winter morning. "Because our security cameras tell a very different story. You logged into the lab at 3:17 a.m." She let the words sink in as the tension in the room climbed to nearly unbearable levels.

James swallowed audibly, his Adam's apple bobbing like a yo-yo. The sensors registered his heart rate spiking dangerously high. "I... I must've forgotten. Yes, that's it," he said, his voice cracking. "I remembered I needed to check some test results."

"At three in the morning?" Mikko's voice rumbled through the room like thunder over a stormy sea. "The same night research data worth millions disappeared?" His words hung heavy in the air, laden with unspoken accusations.

James's hands now trembled so violently that they could barely rest on the tabletop. Sweat poured down his temples in rivulets, and his breathing came in short, panicked gasps that echoed in the sterile quiet of the room.

After forty-five minutes of intense interrogation, where every second felt like an eternity, they had collected enough data. James's story had crumbled piece by piece under the relentless pressure, like a house of cards in a hurricane.

"Let's move to Marcus," Fredrika said as they exited the room, her heels clicking decisively against the floor. "He'll be even more nervous after being forced to wait." Her words hung in the air like a premonition of what was to come.

They were about to enter the right interrogation room when disaster struck. A dark silhouette materialized outside the window, a shadow blacker than the night itself. The reinforced glass shattered inward in a cascade of glittering crystals, refracting light into a thousand rainbows.

The muffled pop of a silenced gunshot followed instantly by the grotesque bloom of crimson on Marcus Thorn's chest, directly over his heart, froze time itself.

Marcus's eyes widened in shock and incomprehension before he slowly, almost gracefully, collapsed onto the cold steel table. Mikko leapt with feline agility toward the shattered window while Freya simultaneously drew her Sig Sauer in a blur of motion. But the dark figure had already dissolved into the night, vanishing like a nightmare at dawn.

Inside the room, Marcus Thorn lay motionless as a dark pool of blood slowly spread beneath his lifeless body. The rhythmic drip of blood onto the polished floor echoed in a hypnotic cadence, a macabre mockery of their efforts.

23

Malmoe, Sweden

Glass shards crunched like ice under Fredrika's feet as she rushed to the fallen Marcus. Blood pulsed from the wound in his chest, forming a widening dark-red circle that seeped relentlessly into his light-blue Ralph Lauren shirt, now a grotesque canvas of life ebbing away. His eyes were wide open in shock, pupils dilated under the fluorescent office lights, while his lips desperately formed words that choked in his throat. "Freya, call 112! Now!" Fredrika's voice cut through the cold night air like a blade, her hands—steadier than her racing heart—pressing firmly against the pulsing wound. "Tell them we have a gunshot victim at Turning Torso, 43rd floor. Say we're with Novus, and it's a Code Red Sapphire."

Mikko, his powerful silhouette outlined against Malmö's glittering skyline, was already at the shattered window. The biting December wind howled into the modern conference room, sending papers on the polished glass table into a chaotic dance. In the pale moonlight, refracted off the building's titanium façade, he could make out a dark figure descending the curved exterior with inhuman precision.

"The shooter's rappelling down the west side!" His voice was controlled but urgent as he grabbed a pair of well-worn tactical gloves from his vest. The familiar scent of Cordura and leather mingled with the metallic tang of blood saturating the room. Fredrika looked up, her hands now slick with Marcus's blood, which glistened under the cold LED ceiling lights. The coppery scent churned her stomach. "Stop him! Freya, as soon as you've called—follow in the car. Grab a walkie-talkie. Stay in constant contact! We can't lose him!"

Mikko didn't hesitate. With his gloves securely on, he gripped the black military-grade rope still dangling from the shattered window frame and swung himself into the night. The wind whistled a primal warning in his ears as he descended the twisting façade of Turning Torso, Malmö stretching out beneath him like an electrified sea of pulsing lights.

Freya was already sprinting toward the elevator, her footsteps echoing like drumbeats against the marble floor of the silent corridor. "Ambulance en route!" she shouted, her voice bouncing off the walls just before the chrome elevator doors closed with a muted hiss.

Meanwhile, Fredrika pressed harder against Marcus's wound, feeling his body temperature drop beneath her hands. "Hold on," she whispered, more command than plea. "Help is on its way."

Down on the street, Mikko landed with a controlled thud on the frost-covered asphalt. The dark figure was already fifty meters away, running toward Lilla Varvsgatan with a precision that betrayed years of training. Mikko broke into a full sprint, his well-trained muscles working in perfect unison for maximum speed. The gap closed steadily, meter by meter, his breath forming small clouds in the frigid air.

Suddenly, the shooter veered toward a waiting black BMW M5, its glossy finish reflecting the streetlights like a mirror. Mikko was just twenty meters behind when the car door slammed shut with a heavy thud and the German V8 roared to life like a roused predator. The tires screeched in protest against the cold asphalt as the car launched forward, leaving black skid marks on the road.

"Damn it!" Mikko spun around, his sharp eyes scanning the sparsely populated street for an alternative. Thirty meters away, an older Kawasaki Ninja stood parked, its green paint dulled by the streetlights. His years of special forces training came into play as he quickly exposed the ignition wires beneath the tank. Within seconds of precise manipulation, the Japanese machine roared to life, its hungry growl reverberating off the building façades.

Freya emerged from the garage in a sleek black Audi RS6, the discreet Novus emblem barely visible against the car's side. She spotted Mikko on the motorcycle and braked sharply beside him in a controlled skid.

"They turned right toward Västra Hamnen!" he shouted over the engine's roar, twisting the throttle. The motorcycle snarled like a wounded beast as he surged after the fleeing car, Freya close behind in the powerful German sedan, its LED headlights slicing through the darkness.

High above, in the interrogation room, Fredrika fought to keep Marcus alive as the approaching ambulance sirens began to wail faintly in the distance, like a distant wolf's call. She pressed the walkie-talkie closer to her mouth with her bloodied hand, leaving a crimson smear on the black plastic. "Status?"

"Pursuit in progress," Freya's focused voice crackled through the radio. "They're heading toward the harbor. Traffic is light. We have a chance."

The night had just begun, and over Malmö's harbor, dark clouds gathered as silent witnesses to the drama unfolding below.

24

Malmoe, Sweden

The engines roared through Malmö's nighttime streets as the black BMW hurtled down Västergatan like a missile, with Mikko close behind on the stolen Kawasaki. The glow of the streetlights turned into streaks of light at their breakneck speed, the contours of the city blurring into the periphery. Freya's RS6 held steady a few car lengths back, her headlights slicing through the darkness like sharp knives.

"Status!" Fredrika's sharp voice cut through the comm system, her words clipped and tense. In the background, muffled voices of paramedics could be heard attending to Marcus on the 43rd floor.

"They're heading north on Neptunigatan!" Mikko's breathless voice broke through the radio. He leaned deeply over the motorcycle's tank as they veered toward Malmö Central, the tires squealing against the asphalt. The cold night air bit into his jacket like icy daggers. "Two people in the car. Driver's skilled."

"Confirmed professional," Freya added quickly as her RS6 weaved through sparse traffic with surgical precision. "Driving patterns match training. They know what they're doing."

The fleeing car suddenly swerved into the opposite lane, forcing a taxi to veer away, before accelerating toward the Carlsgatan intersection. Mikko stayed on their tail, adrenaline pumping through his veins. His SIG Sauer P226 bounced heavily against his thigh in its holster, but at this speed, taking a shot was out of the question.

"Holding position from behind," Freya reported, her RS6 gliding through traffic with smooth precision. "Police have been notified."

"There's no response from Marcus," Fredrika cut in, her voice tightly controlled. "Paramedics are... wait." A brief pause followed, then muffled voices. "They're taking him to SUS. I'll follow shortly. Priority is to capture the shooter alive. We need answers."

The BMW skidded sharply right at the next intersection, its tires leaving black streaks on the asphalt. Mikko had to lean the motorcycle so low that his knee pads scraped against the ground to stay with them. Moments later, the car swerved left again in what was clearly an attempt to force Mikko toward the curb.

"Careful!" Freya's warning came a second too late. Mikko was forced to veer hard to the right, narrowly avoiding a parked car by mere millimeters.

"Mikko! Status!" Freya's voice was laced with urgency.

"Still here," he gritted out between clenched teeth. "They're trying to take me out. Definitely pros."

"Maintain distance," Fredrika ordered. "Freya, can you take the lead?"

"Negative," Freya replied. "Mikko's more maneuverable on the bike."

The chase continued north, past the old shipyard district where modern apartment buildings rose like silent witnesses to the drama unfolding below. The BMW accelerated further, its V8 engine roaring like a wounded animal as the speedometer climbed past 160 kilometers per hour.

"They're heading for the highway!" Mikko shouted, his voice nearly drowned out by the wind. "If they hit the E6, we'll lose them!"

"Not a chance," Freya muttered, her RS6 surging forward. "Fredrika, we need reinforcements up north. They'll likely aim for the exits toward Helsingborg or Landskrona."

"Working on it," Fredrika replied, the sound of rapid typing in the background. "Two teams en route. ETA twelve minutes."

Then, it happened. As they approached the highway on-ramp, a lone police car sat idling, its blue lights reflecting off the guardrail. The BMW showed no intention of slowing. Instead, it accelerated further, its engine's roar echoing between the concrete barriers as it blasted past the patrol car at over 180 kilometers per hour.

"Police contact!" Mikko reported, pushing the Kawasaki to its limits, the engine screaming as it echoed off the walls of the overpass.

"Identified!" Freya responded quickly as her RS6 followed. "Patrol 845. I'm handling comms. Apologies for the intrusion!" she added into the radio, more out of habit than necessity.

"Patrol 845 to Central," they heard through their own comms as the police radio crackled in the background. "We've just been overtaken by... uh... I'm not even sure what overtook us."

"Let them stay confused," Fredrika's calm voice cut in. "Novus is coordinating with regional command. Focus on the target."

The BMW reached the highway, accelerating toward the signs for Helsingborg. Mikko crouched even lower over the motorcycle, making himself as aerodynamic as possible while the wind howled in his ears. His sidearm was useless in this situation—firing a shot at these speeds would be sheer madness.

"Fuel status?" Fredrika demanded sharply.

"Critical," Mikko replied after a quick glance at the gauge. "Less than a quarter tank. This bike wasn't fully fueled when we... borrowed it."

"Options?" Fredrika's tone shifted to command mode—short, precise, and demanding solutions.

"I have an idea," Freya said, her voice taking on a calculating edge that made both Mikko and Fredrika pause. "But it's insane. Mikko, can you get closer to them?"

Mikko swallowed hard, sensing the weight of his teammates' unspoken concerns through the brief silence. "I'll try. What's the plan?"

"Something really stupid," Freya admitted, her RS6 accelerating to close the gap. "Really, *really* stupid."

"Define 'stupid,'" Fredrika's voice snapped with authority.

"I'll explain later," Freya replied curtly. "You'll just try to stop me."

Ahead of them, the BMW carved through the night like a black projectile, its taillights glowing like malevolent red eyes in the darkness. Behind them, the city shrank in the rearview mirrors while the endless black ribbon of the highway stretched toward the horizon.

In Turning Torso's control room, Fredrika pressed her bloodied hands against the desk, her eyes locked on the GPS markers moving across the screen in front of her. She was acutely aware that her team's lives hinged on the decisions made in the next few minutes.

25

Malmoe, Sweden

"My plan is to box them in on both sides," Freya's voice remained steady despite the gravity of the situation. She gripped the RS6's wheel tighter, feeling the texture of the carbon fiber under her gloves. "When I overtake them on the right, they'll try to block me. That's your window, Mikko. Force them into the median while they're focused on me."

"That's too risky," Fredrika's voice crackled through the comms, sharp with worry. The metallic undertone of the radio couldn't mask her concern. "At this speed, the slightest mistake—"

"We don't have a choice," Freya interrupted, shifting the RS6 into position behind the BMW. The speedometer danced over 200 kilometers per hour. "Mikko is almost out of fuel, and if they cross into Denmark, we'll lose our only lead on who ordered the hit on Marcus."

"Confirmed critical fuel level," Mikko's breathless voice broke through, strained from the cold and speed. "Maybe five minutes, max. I'm in. Give the signal."

Freya licked her dry lips, her fingers clenching around the wheel. The RS6's engine purred like a well-tuned predator as she slid into the left lane. The rhythmic alternation of darkness and light from the streetlamps played over the car: shadow, glow, shadow, glow.

The BMW's driver reacted as predicted—a sharp swerve that caused the wide rear tires to momentarily lose grip. But the driver's skill was exceptional, correcting the fishtail with the precision of someone with years of experience.

"Now!" Freya's shout rang through the comms.

Mikko surged forward on the motorcycle, leaning so low his knee guard nearly scraped the asphalt. At the same time, Freya nudged the RS6 toward the BMW's right side. For a fleeting moment—a hopeful, exhilarating moment—the plan worked.

The fleeing car was caught between them and the massive median barrier.

The shots came without warning.

Three sharp cracks pierced through the roar of the engines. Freya caught the muzzle flashes from the BMW's passenger seat a split second before her side window exploded into a shower of safety glass. She instinctively ducked, her head dipping below the dashboard. The RS6 wavered, its tires screaming in protest.

"Freya!" Fredrika's panicked voice echoed through the comms. "Freya, respond!"

"Hit?" Mikko's voice was tight with worry as he struggled to maintain control of the motorcycle.

"Unharmed," Freya gritted out, her hands trembling as she righted the car. "But we lost them. Damn it!"

Ahead, the towering pylons of the Øresund Bridge loomed against the night sky, rising like modern colossi. Their steel cables glinted in the moonlight, a shimmering web of engineering marvel. The BMW raced up the bridge's incline, its V8 engine roaring triumphantly as exhaust flames flared like tiny infernos.

"Two semis, 500 meters ahead," Mikko reported, pushing the motorcycle to its limits while the fuel gauge blinked an ominous red. "They're side by side, blocking both lanes."

It was then the BMW's passenger made his move. Leaning out of the window, he aimed a compact assault rifle with practiced precision. The muzzle flashes lit up the night like erratic lightning, the gunshots echoing off the bridge's steel structure. The front semi's tires exploded in rapid succession. Freya watched it unfold in slow motion: the massive truck veered wildly as the driver fought to regain control. But at that speed, with destroyed tires, the effort was futile. The semi jackknifed, slamming into the guardrail with a force that sent shockwaves through the bridge. Sparks cascaded as metal ground against metal in a deafening crescendo of destruction.

"Left!" Mikko shouted.

"Right!" Freya responded instantly.

They split to either side of the wreck, narrowly avoiding disaster. As they cleared the chaos, they both saw it—the fleeing car abandoned in the middle of the bridge, its doors flung open, the engine idling.

"They're abandoning the vehicle!" Mikko skidded the motorcycle to a halt. "Two individuals heading toward... damn it! They're taking the service door to the pylon!"

"They planned this," Freya growled, leaping out of the RS6 with her service weapon drawn. "The whole route was coordinated."

"Follow them!" Fredrika's command was crystal clear through the comms. "Backup is ten minutes out, but we can't risk losing them now. Be cautious—they're clearly prepared."

Mikko was already moving, taking the narrow spiral staircase inside the pylon two steps at a time. Freya followed close behind, their rapid breaths and pounding footsteps echoing off the cold concrete walls. With every floor they ascended, the air grew thinner and colder.

"They've got... something up there," Freya managed between controlled breaths. "Nobody... runs up a pylon... without a plan."

When they finally burst through the door to the pylon's top platform, the arctic wind hit them like a physical wall. Standing 203.5 meters above the black waters of the Øresund, the world felt surreal. The city sparkled in the distance, while below, the bridge's lights pulsed like a string of pearls through the night. The gunman and his driver stood at the platform's edge, their black parachutes already strapped on. The moonlight gleamed off their gear.

"Stop where you are!" Mikko's voice was almost lost to the howling wind as he leveled his SIG Sauer at the men. "It's over!"

The driver turned to face them, his smile cold and calculating. Without a word, he leaned backward off the edge, disappearing into the abyss like a seasoned BASE jumper.

The gunman—Marcus's shooter—prepared to follow. But Mikko was already moving, his trained muscles propelling him into a sprint.

"Mikko, no!" Freya's desperate scream was swallowed by the roaring wind as Mikko lunged forward, grabbing the shooter's parachute harness just as the man stepped into the void.

For a moment, time froze. Suspended in the air, illuminated by the bridge's spotlights, they were like a macabre sculpture hanging between life and death.

Then they plummeted.

Freya raced to the edge, her heart pounding so fiercely it drowned out the wind. Far below, she saw two parachutes open against the black void of the sea. One carried two figures, spinning wildly in the harsh northern wind.

"Fredrika," her voice wavered as she pressed her communicator, her fingers stiff from cold and adrenaline. "Mikko is... We need water patrols immediately. Two chutes descending, one carrying double. Bearing southwest from pylon four."

The unforgiving wind lashed around her as she stood helplessly atop the pylon, watching the parachutes disappear into the darkness. In the east, dawn began to paint the sky in blood-red hues, but here, at the highest point between Denmark and Sweden, Freya stood alone, watching her partner vanish into the void with the man they had been chasing.

"Hold on, Mikko," she whispered into the night, her words lost to the wind. "Just hold on."

Below, the wail of sirens cut through the dark as police boats sped toward the falling figures, their blue lights reflecting on the icy waters, ready to embrace the men in its frigid depths.

26

Malmoe, Sweden

The icy wind howled through Mikko's clothes as he and the gunman tumbled through the December night. His fingers, already numb from the cold, were locked around the parachute harness like a hydraulic vise. Every muscle fiber in his body worked to maintain his grip as they plunged toward the black waters 200 meters below. The lights of the Øresund Bridge reflected on the waves like slithering silver serpents.

"Let go, you crazy bastard!" the gunman bellowed, his words whipped away by the roaring wind. He lashed out with a backward kick aimed at Mikko's knee, but Mikko, trained for such scenarios at the Swedish Armed Forces Survival School, held firm.

"You're done," Mikko growled through gritted teeth. "It's over." When the parachute deployed, they were yanked upward with a force that darkened Mikko's vision. Pain seared through his shoulders as his joints protested the sudden strain, but sheer adrenaline and survival instinct kept his frozen fingers clenched around the harness.

A piercing scream tore through the wind. Mikko twisted his head and saw the second parachute spinning wildly in the turbulent air around the pylon. The driver's desperate attempts to stabilize himself were futile. The unforgiving wind currents dragged him into a brutal spiral, slamming him into the massive concrete structure. The collision was horrifying. Mikko caught the sight of the man's body crumpling, the sound of the deadly impact drowned by the howling gale.

"Shit! Shit! Shit!" the gunman cursed, his professional veneer beginning to crack as they drifted downward toward the strait. "You don't know what you're doing. You're going to kill us both!"

"Not if you cooperate," Mikko snapped. Below them, he could make out a boat waiting in the water, its faint navigation lights barely visible in the darkness. A Targa 27, Mikko's trained eye noted. Fast and agile. Ideal for a quick escape across the strait. The impact was catastrophic. They hit the boat's deck with a force that sent the world exploding into a supernova of pain. Mikko heard and felt the gunman's leg shatter with a sickening crunch. His own right hand, still clamped around the harness in a cramped death grip, smashed against the railing. The sound of bones fracturing and tendons tearing drew a guttural scream from his throat.

"Jesus Christ, oh my God!" The boat's captain, a wiry man with a weathered and scarred face, backed toward the wheelhouse, his hands trembling. "This wasn't... they said it'd be simple! Just wait here, pick them up. They promised it'd be easy!"

Mikko rolled onto his side, fighting the waves of fiery pain coursing through his body. With his uninjured left hand, he drew his SIG Sauer and leveled it at the captain. His voice was hoarse but steady. "Don't move."

The gunman lay beside him on the slick deck, his expensive black jumpsuit now glistening with sweat and blood. His face twisted in pain, but his eyes... his eyes remained cold and calculating, like a cobra ready to strike.

"You might as well finish it," the gunman hissed through gritted teeth. "I'll never give you what you want."

"Who gave the order?" Mikko forced the words out, struggling to steady the gun with his left hand while the shattered remains of his right throbbed with relentless agony. "Who ordered Marcus's murder?"

A laugh bubbled up from the gunman's throat, sharp and bitter, echoing across the water. "You're so... pathetically ignorant," he sneered. His eyes glittered dangerously in the dim light. "You have no idea what you've stumbled into, do you? The forces you're challenging?"

"Names," Mikko demanded, pressing the muzzle of the gun against the man's chest. "Now."

"Malaconda Villareal," the gunman spat, his voice dripping with disdain. "Sends his regards." A manic grin spread across his face. "The Shadow Council has plans beyond what your little brain could ever comprehend."

Mikko felt the blood in his veins turn to ice. The Shadow Council. A name whispered in the darkest corners of the underworld, a myth to some, a nightmare to others.

"Why Marcus?" Mikko pushed, his voice low and urgent. "What did he discover?"

"Too much." The gunman's grin widened, a hint of madness creeping into his expression. "Far, far too much." His hand moved suddenly, darting toward a hidden pocket in his harness.

"Stop!" Mikko raised the gun, but his reflexes were dulled by pain and cold.

In one fluid motion, the gunman brought something small and black to his lips—a capsule no larger than a pill. His grin turned triumphant. "See you in hell, Novus scum."

"No!" Mikko lunged forward, but it was too late. The convulsions began instantly. The gunman's body arched unnaturally, white foam spilling from his mouth. His wide, staring eyes rolled back in his head. It was over in less than ten seconds.

"Jesus, Mary, and Joseph," the captain muttered, sinking to the deck, his face ashen in the faint navigation lights. His voice shook uncontrollably. "They... they said it was just a transport job. One hour, they said. A year's pay for one hour... I didn't... oh God..."

"Freya," Mikko activated his communicator with trembling fingers, his voice thick with pain and exhaustion. "The target is... the target is eliminated. Suicide. Some sort of fast-acting poison. But we have names. Malaconda Villareal." He swallowed hard, his voice growing heavier. "And the Shadow Council. It's... it's bigger than we thought."

The silence that followed was thick with implications. When Fredrika's voice finally came through, it was hard as steel.

"Understood. Hold your position. Rescue boats are en route. And Mikko... impressive work. Rest now. This is only the beginning."

Mikko slumped against the railing, his shattered hand radiating agony in time with his heartbeat. Above him, the Øresund Bridge loomed like a titanic shadow against the breaking dawn, its lights a string of pearls against the paleening sky. Somewhere up there, Freya stood waiting, while the wail of approaching rescue boats echoed across the dark waters.

His gaze drifted to the dead gunman. Even in death, the man's face retained its cold, knowing smirk, as if in his final moments, he still held a secret that Mikko couldn't grasp. As if this was just the overture to a much darker symphony.

And as the first rescue boat cut through the dark, its powerful spotlight piercing the creeping mist over the strait, Mikko couldn't shake the feeling that they had just opened a door to something far deeper and darker than they had ever imagined. But the only answer was the howling wind and the distant sirens echoing over the cold, black waters.

27

Paris, France

The antique Baccarat chandelier cast a honeyed glow over Malaconda Villareal's private study in his 18th-century apartment. The early morning light filtered through the tall windows, adorned with handwoven silk curtains from Lyon, making the intricate patterns of the Persian silk rug shimmer in deep burgundy and midnight blue. In the open fireplace, a meticulously arranged fire crackled, releasing a subtle scent of applewood into the room.

Jani stood discreetly by the hearth, her elegant silhouette reflected in the Venetian mirror above the mantel. The black Chanel suit she wore blended almost seamlessly with the shadows. She observed in silence as Malaconda finished his morning coffee, the delicate Limoges porcelain clinking softly as he placed the cup on the marble-inlaid side table.

"The secure room is prepared, sir," she said in her characteristically soft accent, a blend of Hungarian origins and Swiss refinement. "All encryption protocols are activated and verified. Dual-layer security."

Malaconda nodded, the movement barely perceptible. His dark suit, custom-tailored on Savile Row, was flawless as always. Every seam and detail spoke of generations of power and influence. Rising with an effortless authority that came from a lifetime of decisions made in the shadows, he walked toward a concealed door hidden behind a French walnut bookshelf.

"No interruptions during the call," he instructed, his voice calm yet absolute. "No matter what happens. No matter who arrives."

Behind the bookshelf lay the secure communications room, a high-tech fortress embedded within the historic building's meter-thick stone walls. Here, history gave way to stark functionality and cutting-edge technology. The walls were lined with carbon fiber composites and advanced signal jamming systems. Malaconda seated himself before the holographic display just as it hummed to life, pulsing faintly with an electrical hum.

Dr. Shinkelhof's avatar materialized in the room, a ghostly projection of millions of flickering light particles. The Austrian's usually composed demeanor was frayed—small muscle twitches at the jawline and a barely perceptible tremor in his left hand betrayed his stress.

"Villareal." Shinkelhof's voice carried the distorted quality of multiple encryption layers but retained its sharp, precise tone. "We have a situation requiring immediate attention."

Leaning back in his handcrafted desk chair, Malaconda studied the hologram with an intensity that made Shinkelhof adjust his cravat instinctively. "Proceed."

"BioVita... the project demanded immediate action. The window was shrinking by the hour." Shinkelhof paused, swallowing hard before continuing with forced confidence. "I authorized the use of Gavrail to handle the situation."

The room's temperature seemed to drop several degrees. When Malaconda spoke again, his voice was low, controlled, but edged with an icy fury that made the air hum with tension.

"You did what?" His fingers rested on the black quartzite tabletop, curling into a tight fist. "You deployed one of our top operatives without consulting the Council? Without even informing me? Do you comprehend the risk you've taken? This is scandalous. You are a new member of the Shadow Council; you cannot act without my consent."

"The situation was urgent," Shinkelhof replied, holding his head high despite the accusation in Malaconda's tone. Sweat glistened on his brow in the hologram's bluish glow. "BioVita's research... its potential was too great to ignore."

"Silence!" Malaconda's hand slammed against the table, the impact sending a ripple through the holographic displays. "You've jeopardized decades of meticulous planning with your impulsive actions. Novus now knows our name. Our shield of anonymity is cracking like an eggshell under a hammer."

Something in Shinkelhof's posture, however, gave Malaconda pause. There was a defiance there, an unexpected strength. A hunger that echoed something deeply familiar—a reflection of himself.

"Explain," Malaconda said after a long silence, the hum of the surrounding technology filling the room. "Explain what compelled you to make this... extraordinary decision."

And Shinkelhof explained. Words poured out of him like a dam breaking, revealing how BioVita was on the brink of collapse and how its invention could salvage its future. He spoke of a compromised scientist within the company, of a month-long operation to secure assets. He described his plan to use both Prometheus's Eye and Dr. Rossi with Genesis's Eye during a staged press conference to save BioVita's reputation and finances. The urgency of the closing time window had demanded action, or so he believed.

As Malaconda listened, a grudging respect began to stir within him—an admiration he hadn't anticipated. Here was a man who had seized an opportunity, bypassed bureaucracy, and taken calculated risks to protect a vision. It struck Malaconda with sudden clarity: this was precisely how the Shadow Council had begun generations ago. Not with cautious deliberations in shadowed rooms, but with bold, calculated gambles made in moments of necessity.

"This will cost you," Malaconda said finally, his tone thoughtful rather than accusatory. Rising, he paced slowly around the hologram. "The Shadow Council was built on daring, yes, but also on precision. On patience. On knowing when to strike and when to wait in the shadows."

"I understand." Shinkelhof inclined his head gravely. "And I am prepared to pay the price, whatever it may be."

Malaconda stopped by the window, his silhouette a dark shadow against the golden morning light now spilling over the rooftops of Paris. "We will manage this," he said, turning slowly back to face the hologram. "But from now on, Shinkelhof, you will coordinate such actions with the Council. With me. Understood?"

"Of course." Shinkelhof's slight bow carried an air of old-world courtesy. "And… thank you, Villareal. For your understanding."

As the hologram faded, Malaconda remained motionless, lost in thought. Outside, the city stirred to life, oblivious to the drama unfolding in the elegant rooms of Place Vendôme. He found a strange poetry in the situation. Shinkelhof's impatience and courage mirrored the very hunger that had once driven the Council's founders. The same relentless will to shape the world rather than wait for the world to shape itself.

Opening the door, he found Jani standing precisely where he'd left her, silent and efficient as a shadow.

"Contact our operatives in Malmö," he instructed, moving toward his Louis XV desk. "And secure a line to our contacts within Novus. It's time to clean up." He paused, a faint smile playing on his lips. "And Jani… schedule a meeting with the Council. It's time they learned of Dr. Shinkelhof's… initiative."

Outside the windows, Paris awoke in a symphony of light and sound, unaware of the power plays unfolding in the rooms above. As the morning sun draped the city in a veil of gold, Malaconda Villareal, with centuries of clandestine power in his veins, began weaving the next intricate thread in the Shadow Council's vast tapestry of ambition, influence, and secrets.

28

Malmoe, Sweden

The rain pattered against the hospital window in an endless stream, creating blurry patterns in the reflections of Malmö's city center. The yellow streetlights, muted by the downpour, cast a dim glow, making the city look like an abstract painting in gold and gray. Madeleine Singh stood by the fogged glass, her hand resting lightly on the cold surface. The thin hospital gown offered little protection from the chill emanating from the window. Midnight approached, but sleep felt like a distant possibility despite the painkillers coursing through her system. The room at Malmö General was spartan but comfortable, with cream-colored walls and practical furnishings. The unmistakable scent of disinfectant and freshly laundered sheets mingled with the faint perfume of the flower arrangement her team had sent—lilies and white roses in a discreet glass vase. The IV stand beside her bed cast long shadows across the polished linoleum floor, a constant reminder of how close it had been. Too close.

"Who?" she whispered into the darkness, her fingers unconsciously reaching for the wound at her side. Through the bandage, she could feel the warmth of the healing injury. "Who among you turned against everything we built? Everything we fought for?"

Twenty years. Twenty years of her life had been dedicated to building Novus from the ground up. From a vision born out of despair and loss into an organization that made a real difference. Every agent handpicked, every operation meticulously planned. She had trained them, shaped them, trusted them like family. And now...

A soft knock interrupted her thoughts. The door opened carefully, and a nurse in a midnight-blue uniform stepped in. Maria, if Madeleine remembered correctly from earlier shifts. The woman carried the calm authority Madeleine often saw in seasoned agents.

"Miss Singh? I noticed your light was still on." Maria's voice was warm, her soft Scanian accent evoking memories of home-cooked meals and childhood comforts. "Can't sleep? Understandable, after what you've been through."

Madeleine offered a faint smile, turning away from the window. "Too much on my mind. The thoughts won't rest."

Maria approached the window, standing beside her. Her shoes made barely a sound on the floor—a result of years spent moving quietly through hospital corridors. "Rain has a soothing quality, don't you think? Like it's washing away the day's troubles."

"How long have you worked here, Maria?" Madeleine studied the nurse's profile, noting the fine lines around her eyes that spoke of both laughter and worry.

"Twenty-five years in January." Maria, too, gazed out at the rain, her hands clasped loosely in front of her. "I've seen much in that time. Lives beginning, lives ending. Triumphs and tragedies. You learn to value every moment."

"That sounds like wisdom from someone who knows what they're talking about." Madeleine felt an unexpected kinship with this woman, who had also dedicated her life to helping others.

"When you've seen as much as we do here..." Maria paused, choosing her words carefully. "You realize how fragile it all is. How precious every day, every meeting, every smile truly is. Sometimes we forget that in the stress of daily life and the chase for goals. But in the end, it's the small moments that matter most."

"Yes..." Madeleine thought of her team, the morning briefings, the late-night strategy sessions. "It's easy to lose perspective when chasing your ambitions. To forget what really matters."

"You should try to rest," Maria said gently, touching Madeleine's arm lightly. "Your body heals better with sleep. And your thoughts will be clearer in the morning."

After Maria left, her soft footsteps fading into the corridor, the restlessness under Madeleine's skin grew unbearable. The sterile room felt suddenly stifling. The walls seemed to inch closer, pressing in on her. She needed to be back, needed to be where her team needed her most.

She grabbed the remote from the bedside table and turned on the TV, keeping the volume low to avoid disturbing the quiet night. A live broadcast on TV4 immediately caught her attention. The reporter stood at the base of the Øresund Bridge, his rain-slicked jacket gleaming in the camera's light.

"...dramatic scenes in central Malmö earlier tonight as a high-speed chase through the city culminated in an extraordinary incident on the Øresund Bridge. Witnesses report high speeds and gunfire. A truck reportedly crashed, and unconfirmed reports mention individuals parachuting off the bridge. Police remain tight-lipped but have confirmed that—"

Madeleine's hand instinctively reached for her phone. She dialed the number from memory, her fingers moving as if by their own will.

"Fredrika here." The voice on the other end was tired but alert, the professional tone barely masking the stress beneath.

"Tell me everything."

A short pause filled with heavy silence. "Marcus was shot on the 43rd floor. He's stable now, but..." Fredrika inhaled deeply, steadying herself. "It's more complicated than we first thought. The shooter is dead, but we have names. Malaconda Villareal. And something called the Shadow Council."

Madeleine felt her blood turn to ice. The room seemed suddenly colder. "The Shadow Council? Are you absolutely sure about that name?"

A pause. "Absolutely. Mikko..." Another pause, heavier this time. "Mikko is injured but okay. Crushed hand. He got the name from the shooter before... before he took his own life."

"I'll be there tomorrow."

"Madeleine, you need rest. The doctors said—"

"Tomorrow, Fredrika." Her tone brooked no argument, carrying the same steely authority she used when training recruits. "Have the team assembled by nine. We can't afford to lose more time. Not now."

After the call ended, Madeleine stood by the window, staring into the night. The rain had intensified, hammering harder against the glass in a growing crescendo. **The Shadow Council.** A name she had hoped never to hear again, a ghost from the past refusing to stay buried.

She glanced at the IV stand, at the white walls trying to confine her, at the monitors pulsing in time with her heartbeat.

Tomorrow she would be back where she was needed. Tomorrow the hunt would begin in earnest.

Twenty years of work was at stake. Somewhere out there, a traitor threatened to tear down everything they had built, everything they had fought for, everything they had sacrificed so much to create.

"Let the game begin," she whispered into the night as the rain continued its relentless drumming against the window, promising a storm ahead. "This time, it ends differently."

Beneath her hospital gown, the scar from an old gunshot burned—a constant reminder of the price of trust. History had a tendency to repeat itself. But this time, she would be ready.

29

Rome, Italy

The intensive care unit at Ospedale San Camillo was steeped in the characteristic dimness of hospitals at night. The muted sounds of medical equipment—the rhythmic beeping of the heart monitor, the soft hiss of the oxygen apparatus, the distant clicking of the IV pump—melded with the low hum of the air conditioning. Through the tall hospital windows, Rome's skyline glimmered, the city's eternal lights reflecting off the modern glass façades opposite.

Dr. Elena Rossi lay motionless in her hospital bed, her usually animated face pale against the stark white sheets. The thick bandage covering her left eye was a stark reminder of the attack she had endured. Thin tubes and wires connected her to monitoring equipment, rendering her oddly vulnerable—a sharp contrast to the commanding scientist they had met before.

Hugo stood at the foot of the bed, his hand resting on the cold metal railing as he observed the monitor displaying her vital signs. Sussie sat in the worn visitor's chair beside her, her gaze alternating between Dr. Rossi and the pulsing screen that recorded every heartbeat, every breath.

"I should have told you earlier," Dr. Rossi's voice was weak, barely more than a whisper breaking the sterile silence. "About the prototypes... about everything." Her hand drifted unconsciously to the bandage, her fingers trembling slightly.

"The Genesis prototype—the one I carry—was our first breakthrough. But Prometheus..." She paused, swallowing hard as the monitor registered an uptick in her pulse. "Prometheus was something entirely different. The perfected version. And now they have it."

Hugo and Sussie exchanged a swift glance over the bed. Suddenly, the small details they had noticed before clicked into place—the subtle movements, the faint delay in her left eye's reactions, the unusual reflections under certain lighting conditions.

"How long have you had Genesis?" Hugo asked.

"Three years, two months, and fourteen days," Dr. Rossi replied, closing her right eye, exhaustion etched across her face. "It was the only way... the only way to develop Prometheus. I lost my eye in the same lab fire that took Marco's sight. It felt... it felt like fate somehow, to use myself as the first test subject for Genesis. That experience led to the breakthrough with Prometheus."

A monitor beeped rhythmically in the background as she continued, "Shinkelhof..." Her voice hardened at the name. "He wanted both prototypes, especially Prometheus, and also me and my expertise. He didn't just offer money for the research. He promised to help Marco, to give him the Prometheus implant immediately. But I saw it... saw it in his eyes during our last meeting. That glint of... something cold. Something calculating. He would use the technology for entirely different purposes."

"What purposes?" Hugo pressed gently, stepping closer to the head of the bed.

"Surveillance. Control. Total surveillance." Her grip on Sussie's hand tightened, her knuckles whitening. "Genesis is limited, but Prometheus... Imagine the scenario—millions of people with Prometheus implants. Every visual input potentially monitored, analyzed, stored. A perfect surveillance device disguised as medical aid."

She paused, gathering her thoughts. "But there's a reason we never released Prometheus for clinical trials. The neural processor is too powerful, too complex. Genesis uses a simpler architecture that is entirely safe—it naturally integrates with the brain's visual cortex. But Prometheus..." Her hand moved unconsciously toward her own implant. "Its neural interface requires precise calibration. Without the correct synchronization codes, it risks overstimulating the optic nerve, creating uncontrollable neural loops. We saw it in our early tests—before we developed the safety protocols."

"How severe are the risks?" Hugo asked.

"Without calibration? Permanent neurological damage. Blindness. Possibly worse." She swallowed hard. "The portable stabilizer can keep the system functional for 48 hours, but after that... And if they try to force a neural connection without the proper protocols..." She shook her head. "They don't understand what they're toying with."

30

Rome, Italy

The shadows stretched long in the narrow alley opposite Ospedale San Camillo. Steam rose from the rain-soaked asphalt, and the air was thick with the mingled scents of nearby restaurant kitchens and the antiseptic tang of the hospital. Gavrail stood motionless beside a graffitied electrical box, his tailored Brioni suit in deepest midnight blue blending perfectly with the gloom. His stance was relaxed yet alert, like a cobra poised to strike.

Next to him, Nico fidgeted with a butterfly knife, the blade flicking open and shut in a hypnotic rhythm. Behind them, Marco and the other two men—Dante and Pietro—kept to the shadows between rusted containers, barely visible in the dim light.

"Hospital routines are beautiful in their predictability," Nico remarked in his characteristic Sicilian accent, his eyes fixed on the staff entrance.

"Silence," Gavrail commanded softly, his voice smooth as cold steel. "We are not here to admire routines." His gray eyes, almost silver in the weak glow of the streetlamps, systematically analyzed every detail of the hospital façade. "The ID cards must remain pristine. No visible marks or bloodstains. Hospital staff are trained to notice such things."

"We know how to handle this," Marco muttered, his hand resting on the custom Beretta holstered beneath his jacket. "This isn't exactly the first time we've—"

"It is the first time with me," Gavrail interrupted, his tone silencing Marco mid-sentence. "And I do not tolerate mistakes." The hours dragged on as the darkness thickened over Rome. Gavrail remained utterly still, an unsettling display of patience that even the seasoned men around him found disconcerting. There was something profoundly unnatural about his unyielding composure, the complete absence of fidgeting or nervous tics.

"What makes him so special?" Pietro whispered to Dante, his voice barely audible over the alley's ambient sounds.

"Don't ask," Dante murmured back, his tone clipped. "Those who ask too much about Gavrail... tend to disappear."

At 11:07 p.m., the side door hissed open with a soft pneumatic sigh. Two doctors in white coats stepped into the night, their conversation about patient records and medications echoing faintly between the walls.

"Now," Gavrail's command was barely louder than a breath. What followed was a display of brutal efficiency. Nico and Marco approached the doctors with a well-rehearsed story about an injured homeless man, leading them deeper into the alley.

Dante and Pietro lurked in the shadows, predators waiting for the signal. No gunshots—silence was paramount. Instead, they worked with calculated blows and knife thrusts. The muffled sounds of breaking bones and stifled cries were absorbed by the alley's walls.

Gavrail observed the process with clinical detachment. "The coats," he ordered when it was done. "And the cards. Now."

Nico wiped the blood from his hands with a black silk handkerchief before handing over the white coats. "That faint mark there," he pointed to an almost imperceptible stain, "could easily pass as coffee. Doctors are notorious for being careless with coffee."

Under the streetlamp, Gavrail inspected the ID cards. Dr. Alessandro Bianchi and Dr. Marco Conti. The photos bore enough resemblance; in the dim hospital lighting, no one would look twice. He studied the details: cardiologist and anesthesiologist. Perfect disguises for moving through the ICU.

"Dante, Pietro—dispose of the evidence thoroughly," he instructed as he donned one of the white coats with fluid precision. "Marco—you and the others establish positions at the east-side emergency exit. If, by some chance, things go awry..."

"Nothing ever goes wrong when you're in charge," Nico interjected, now looking the part in his doctor's coat. "Your... reputation speaks for itself."

A faint smile ghosted across Gavrail's lips. "ICU, fourth floor. Dr. Rossi is in room 412, according to our sources." He glanced at his Breitling Navitimer—a masterpiece of Swiss craftsmanship. "We have exactly twenty-seven minutes until the night round begins. More than sufficient."

They moved toward the hospital's main entrance, their steps purposeful and measured, as though they had walked this path countless times before. Gavrail's posture perfectly mimicked that of an overworked doctor—tired yet professional. The silent ticking of his watch synchronized with his movements, counting down the minutes to the next phase of the operation.

"A flawless surgical procedure requires absolute precision," he murmured as they approached the entrance. "Timing. Focus. And above all..." he tossed the bloodied handkerchief into a trash bin, "...proper cleanup afterward."

"Quite right, Doctor," Nico replied as they passed through the automatic doors. The antiseptic hospital air enveloped them like a cold mist.

Behind them, in the dark alley, Dante and Pietro worked methodically to erase all traces of the night's first "operation," while Marco prepared for the second. The muted sounds of their efforts were swallowed by the night, leaving no evidence of the violence that had occurred.

Inside, the hospital opened up before Gavrail and his men— bright, sterile, and blissfully unaware that two of its wolves had donned the sheep's clothing of healers.

31

Rome, Italy

The pale morning light filtered through the blinds in Dr. Rossi's hospital room at Ospedale San Camillo, casting striped shadows on the linoleum floor. The rhythmic beeping of monitoring equipment blended with the muffled sounds of hospital activity outside. A half-drunk cup of espresso from the hospital cafeteria sat on the bedside table, its rich aroma a sharp contrast to the antiseptic scent that permeated the room.

Dr. Rossi gingerly touched the bandage covering her left eye. "All the source code is embedded in the eye, you understand?" she said with a faint, almost cunning smile. "But my expertise... that resides here." She tapped her right temple. "I ensured it was memorized, an extra safeguard after Shinkelhof's first attempt to acquire the technology."

Hugo leaned forward in the worn visitor's chair, its metal legs scraping softly against the floor. "And Shinkelhof wants both Prometheus, Genesis, and you?"

"Yes. That's why I..." Her words trailed off suddenly, her uninjured eye focusing intently on the door. Footsteps echoed in the corridor—measured, deliberate, and distinct from the hurried pace of typical hospital staff.

Sussie, who had been standing by the window, observing the traffic four stories below, turned toward the door. Her trained instincts immediately registered the irregularity in the rhythm of the approaching steps. "Hugo... something's wrong."

The door opened with controlled precision, and two doctors in immaculate white coats stepped in. The taller one, with silver-gray hair at his temples, consulted a clipboard. "Dr. Rossi, we need to perform a quick check of—"

Time condensed into crystalline moments of realization. Hugo noticed it—the subtle motion as the shorter "doctor" reached inside his coat in a way no real physician would. Hugo's hand instinctively moved toward the weapon concealed under his jacket.

Then, everything erupted in a cacophony of movement and sound.

Hugo dove sideways into a trained roll as the first silenced shot struck the wall with a dull thud, sending a spray of plaster and debris raining down where his head had been milliseconds earlier.

Sussie was already moving, her reflexes as sharp as a predator's. "Dr. Rossi, down!" With a swift motion, she toppled the hospital bed, creating makeshift cover as she drew her SIG Sauer with practiced fluidity.

"No!" Dr. Rossi's voice cut sharply through the adrenaline-fueled chaos as she yanked out her IV line with surprising determination, belying her fragile condition. "Call security!"

A second shot from Gavrail sliced through the air where she had been standing moments before. She rolled to the other side of the overturned bed with remarkable agility. Metal fragments from the bedframe scattered as the bullet struck.

"Impressive reflexes, Doctor," Gavrail's voice was smooth as velvet, cold as steel. "But entirely unnecessary. We need you alive."

Hugo returned fire from behind a medical cart, shattering IV bottles and scattering supplies in a shower of liquid and glass. Nico, the shorter of the two assailants, moved toward the bed with the predatory grace of a trained operative, his every movement honed by years of experience.

Suddenly, the fire alarm blared, triggered by a stray bullet striking a sensor. The corridor outside erupted into a frenzy of panicked voices and hurried footsteps.

"Take her alive!" Gavrail's command cut through the din like a scalpel. "We need her!" His next shot punctured an oxygen tank, filling the air with a sharp hiss of escaping gas.

"Over my dead body," Sussie muttered, squeezing off two precise shots that forced the silver-haired assassin to retreat behind the doorframe. "Hugo! Watch your right flank!"

Hugo caught the movement in his peripheral vision—Nico attempting a classic flanking maneuver. A quick shot from Hugo's weapon sent the Italian diving behind an overturned blood pressure monitor, its screen still flickering faintly.

"They must have backup," Dr. Rossi gasped as she crawled toward the bathroom, a thin line of blood trailing from a superficial cut on her cheek.

Another burst of fire from Gavrail interrupted her, his precision chilling even amidst the chaos. Each shot was calculated to restrict their movement, driving them toward the far corner of the room.

"Alternate exit?" Hugo shouted, rolling aside as another bullet shattered the medical cart, sending a cloud of crushed pills into the air.

"Service elevator!" Dr. Rossi's voice was strained but focused. "Twenty meters down the corridor to the right. There's a keypad, but I—" Her sentence was cut off as the door on the other side of the room burst open.

Black-uniformed security guards stormed in, weapons drawn. "On the ground! Now!"

"Ah, reinforcements." Nico's voice dripped with sarcasm as he tossed a small black cylinder onto the floor. It clinked ominously against the tiles. "Let's raise the stakes."

"Flashbang! Cover your eyes!" Hugo's warning rang out.

The detonation was deafening. Blinding light reflected off the shattered glass fragments, transforming the room into a dizzying carousel of light and shadow. The acrid smell of gunpowder mixed with the burnt plastic odor of fried electronics.

Amid the chaos, Hugo heard Dr. Rossi's panicked scream, followed by the muffled thud of a body hitting the floor. As his vision cleared, he saw Gavrail dragging the struggling scientist toward the door with ruthless efficiency, while Nico laid down suppressive fire with short, controlled bursts.

"Hugo! Left side!" Sussie's shout came too late.

A second flashbang detonated, its force amplified by the confined space. This time, the blast shattered one of the windows, sending shards raining onto the street below.

When the smoke and dust began to settle, Gavrail, Nico, and Dr. Rossi were gone. The only trace of her was a thin smear of blood leading toward the door.

The fire alarm continued its shrill wail as dazed security personnel flooded into the bullet-riddled room. Hugo struggled to his feet, his ears ringing from the explosions. His suit was coated in a fine layer of glass and plaster dust.

"They're taking the service elevator," he rasped into his radio, reloading his weapon. "All available units—"

"It's already too late," Sussie interrupted bitterly, holding up a bloodstained bandage from the floor. "They planned every detail. Every move. This was a perfectly coordinated operation."

Outside, the wail of approaching police sirens echoed as blue lights flickered against the shattered windows. But Hugo and Sussie both knew it was futile.

The hunt had only just begun, and this time, the stakes were higher than ever.

32

Rome, Italy

The interrogation room at Rome's police headquarters was starkly utilitarian, its gray walls and single overhead bulb casting harsh shadows. A surveillance camera blinked red in the corner like an unblinking eye. The early morning sunlight slanted through the blinds, creating sharp geometric patterns on the walls and floor, catching motes of dust swirling in the tense air. Two iced espressos sat untouched on the battered metal table, their aromatic steam mingling with the stale scents of cigarette smoke and antiseptic.

Commissioner Lorenzo Bianchi, a towering man in a tailored navy Armani suit, leaned back in his chair, which groaned under his weight. His dark eyes were skeptical beneath bushy eyebrows that resembled steel wool, and he twirled a Mont Blanc pen idly between his fingers.

"Let me see if I understand this correctly, Signore Xavier," he began, his flawless English weighted with a Tuscan accent, each word deliberate. "You claim that two armed men, disguised as doctors, somehow bypassed our security and attacked a patient at Ospedale San Camillo—one of Italy's most secure hospitals." He paused for dramatic effect. "That this patient was carrying some sort of… how shall we say… experimental cybernetic eye. And that this led to a gunfight which destroyed an entire hospital ward?"

"That's exactly what happened," Hugo replied, his tone professionally neutral despite the irritation simmering beneath the surface. His fingers drummed lightly against the table's edge. "If you would just contact—"

"Signore Xavier," Bianchi interrupted, his voice smooth as olive oil but with a sharp undertone. "We have a respected hospital in chaos. Two security guards with gunshot wounds. Property damage in the millions of euros. And you expect me to believe this is about something that sounds like science fiction? A magical eye?" He smirked skeptically. "Perhaps we should also be looking for aliens, hmm?"

Sussie leaned forward, her posture taut like a coiled spring. "Call Novus. Speak with Madeleine Singh. One call is all it will take to verify our story."

"Ah yes, this mysterious organization you claim to represent. This... Novus." He pronounced the name as though it left a bitter taste in his mouth. "Which no one has ever—"

Hugo's hand slammed against the table, the sharp sound making the coffee cups jump. "Call. Her. Now." His voice was low but brimming with unyielding authority.

Something in his tone—perhaps its undeniable certainty—made Bianchi pause. After a long, tense silence, the commissioner reached for the phone, an antiquated relic of polished black plastic. "Give me the number."

Twenty minutes later, the atmosphere in the room had undergone a seismic shift. Bianchi sat rigidly upright, his face pale, beads of sweat forming on his brow as he listened intently to the voice on the other end of the line.

"Yes, Minister..." he stammered, nervously tugging at his tie. "Of course we will... Yes, I understand completely. You have our full cooperation." When he hung up, his demeanor had transformed—humble, almost deferential.

"My superior and Signorina Singh have explained the situation in detail," he said, his voice barely steady. "She... mentioned Venice, 2018." His voice faltered at the mention of the year.

"And?" Sussie pressed, her eyes narrowing like a cat ready to pounce.

"And we are, of course, at your full disposal." He stood so quickly his chair scraped loudly against the floor. "My men are already reviewing the city's surveillance network. We've locked down all major exits from Rome. The entire police force is mobilized."

Hugo's phone buzzed on the table, vibrating with a metallic hum. Fredrika's name lit up the screen like a warning beacon. "Hugo here. Yes, we're... understood." He switched to speaker mode and placed the phone between the coffee cups.

"The situation is critical," Fredrika's crisp voice filled the room. "Madeleine is coming on the line now."

A faint electronic click, then Madeleine's voice—firm, devoid of any trace of her recent injuries. "Hugo, Sussie. We've tracked Gavrail's team to a property in Trastevere, in the old Jewish quarter of Rome. They're moving quickly, likely heading for Termini station. We suspect they'll take a train north toward Germany—Shinkelhof Medical's headquarters are there."

"Orders?" Hugo asked, already rising as adrenaline coursed through his veins.

"Priority one: Locate them. Priority two: Stop them. Dr. Rossi must be rescued alive. The artificial eye is secondary for now." A deliberate pause. "And Hugo... be aware that Gavrail is a ghost. A living legend in certain very dark circles. Be extremely cautious. His kill record makes our worst adversaries look amateur."

"What resources do we have?" Sussie asked, her fingers already flying over her iPad as she downloaded maps of the area.

"Fredrika is coordinating from our mobile command center. A tactical team is twenty minutes out by helicopter, fully armed. Commissioner Bianchi and his special unit will provide ground support." Madeleine's tone hardened, her words edged with steel. "But remember—this is a Novus operation. We can't risk exposing the full extent of Dr. Rossi's research to the wrong people. Keep civilian police and military at arm's length."

"Crystal clear." Hugo turned to Bianchi. "We need your fastest car. And free passage through the city."

Bianchi nodded and spoke into his radio, his hand trembling almost imperceptibly. "Giuseppe, bring up the Quadrifoglio. Notify all units—the two Novus agents have carte blanche. Full authority."

"One more thing," Madeleine's voice cut through like a laser. "There's likely a leak within Novus. Someone gave Gavrail precise timing and location for the attack. Trust no one except each other, Fredrika, and me. Understood?"

"Understood," Hugo and Sussie replied in unison.

"Good." They could almost hear the dangerous smile in Madeleine's voice. "Good luck. And... come back alive. Both of you. That's an order."

As they exited the interrogation room, the morning sun blazed hot over Rome's ancient stonework. Outside, a sleek black Alfa Romeo Giulia Quadrifoglio awaited them, its V6 engine growling impatiently, the polished body gleaming in the sunlight like a predator poised to strike.

"Trastevere," Hugo said, sliding into the driver's seat and feeling the car's raw power vibrate through the steering wheel. "How many potential hideouts?"

"Analyzing now." Sussie's fingers danced across her tablet, data streaming across the screen. "In that part of the city... too many tourists heading to Termini. It's controlled chaos at best."

"Exactly." Hugo smirked grimly as he revved the engine, savoring the aggressive growl. "Which means Gavrail knows exactly what he's doing. He chose this location for a reason." He shifted gears, and the car roared forward like a bullet fired from a gun. "This will be... interesting."

The Alfa Romeo weaved through Rome's morning traffic like a black arrow, its sirens rousing the Eternal City as the sun climbed higher over its ancient domes. The hunt was on, and time was running out for Dr. Rossi.

33

Rome, Italy

Roma Termini loomed like a modern colossus in the morning light, its expansive glass façade reflecting the rising sun in a thousand glittering shards. Early commuters streamed in and out of the automatic doors, their footsteps echoing against the polished marble floors. The aroma of freshly brewed espresso from the station's numerous cafes mingled with the metallic tang of brake dust and faint traces of exhaust.

Gavrail guided the black Mercedes-Benz AMG through the dense morning traffic with surgical precision. His ice-gray eyes scanned the rearview mirror, constantly assessing his surroundings. His gloved hands rested lightly on the wheel, steady and precise—hands trained in both precision and violence.

"Status on the target area?" His voice was low, calm, and unyielding.

"Perimeter secured," Marco's voice crackled through the encrypted radio. "Dante is embedded with station staff. Pietro is on surveillance control."

In the back seat, Dr. Rossi lay slumped, semi-conscious. Blood from the wound on her forehead had begun to crust in the morning heat, leaving a dark, jagged stain on the pale leather upholstery. Nico's improvised pressure dressing, hastily applied during their escape from the hospital, was already saturated.

"Vitals?" Gavrail asked clinically, turning into the underground parking garage beneath the station.

"Seventy BPM, irregular," Nico replied, checking her pulse with practiced efficiency. His other hand rested on the silenced Sig Sauer in his lap.

"She'll survive the trip to Berlin." Gavrail parked the car in a shadowed corner, perfectly concealed from the surveillance cameras. "Dr. Schäfer will have full medical facilities ready."

Dr. Rossi stirred weakly in the back seat, her uninjured eye fluttering open. The bandage over her artificial eye was damp with sweat and blood. "You... don't understand," she rasped, her voice barely audible over the idling engine. "The eye... the implant... it will..."

"Silence," Nico snapped, but Gavrail raised a hand, signaling him to hold.

"What about the eye, Doctor?" Gavrail asked, his tone suddenly softer, an almost perfect facsimile of concern. "Tell us."

"The security protocols..." She coughed, her dry lips flecked with crimson.

"There will be plenty of time for technical explanations later," Gavrail said coolly, switching off the engine with a deliberate twist. "Nico, prepare for transport."

Everything had been planned down to the last detail. A collapsible hospital wheelchair. Crisp, freshly pressed doctor's coats complete with authentic-looking ID badges. Medical charts so convincing they could fool seasoned professionals.

"Stazione prossima, dottore," Nico quipped mockingly as they wheeled the chair through a dim underground passage toward the platforms, his Italian accent deliberately thicker than usual. "Next stop Berlin. Longest patient transfer in history."

Gavrail remained silent, his focus absolute. His eyes scanned every passerby, every security camera, every potential threat. His hand rested lightly on the wheelchair's handles, ready to release it and draw his weapon in a fraction of a second.

They passed through the security checkpoint with effortless ease—the forged medical credentials were masterpieces crafted by the Shadow Council's top document specialists in Hamburg. Station personnel barely glanced at their papers.

"Platform 7 secured," Marco's voice crackled through their hidden earpieces, clear and steady. "Carriage 23 is ready. Dante has neutralized the regular staff."

The sleek ICE train waited like a metallic serpent, its aerodynamic silver body gleaming under the station's fluorescent lights. Dante met them at the carriage door, his Deutsche Bahn uniform so impeccable that even other staff nodded at him in passing.

"Welcome aboard," Dante announced loudly for any eavesdroppers, his German accent flawless. "We've prepared a private cabin specifically for this medical transfer."

Dr. Rossi's hand shot out, gripping Gavrail's arm with surprising strength. Her uninjured eye burned with feverish intensity. "You will never... use it," she hissed, her voice trembling with desperation. "Never. The protocols are designed to—"

Gavrail leaned down, his lips mere millimeters from her ear. "That's precisely why you're coming to Berlin, Doctor," he murmured, his tone as smooth as silk but as cold as winter steel. "To show us how to bypass those protocols."

As they wheeled her into the private cabin, the station's PA system came alive with a series of departure announcements. Gavrail discreetly noted unusual activity on the platform— security personnel moving with a purpose, their steps too coordinated, their earpieces buzzing with communication.

"We have company," he muttered into his concealed mic. "Nico, secure the doctor. Marco, Pietro—initiate diversion protocol Beta."

Dr. Rossi slumped back in the wheelchair, her face pale under the station's harsh fluorescent lighting. The artificial eye beneath the bloodstained bandage pulsed faintly, almost as if reacting to her heightened stress. A bead of sweat trickled down her temple.

"Berlin," Gavrail said softly, sliding the cabin door shut with a quiet *click.* "That's where we'll get all the answers we need. Whether you like it or not."

34

Rome, Italy

The black Alfa Romeo glided through Rome's narrow streets like a prowling panther, its V6 engine purring impatiently as Hugo navigated the labyrinth of ancient alleys. The morning air was already heavy with heat, a mix of freshly baked bread from street bakeries, exhaust fumes, and the unmistakable scent of a city coming to life.

"Fanculo!" An irate taxi driver honked as Hugo sharply swerved to avoid a Vespa. Turning onto Via Cavour, they were met by a solid wall of cars gleaming in the morning sun.

"Damn it," Hugo muttered, tapping the leather-clad steering wheel. His fingers drummed an anxious rhythm as he scanned the traffic for openings. Ahead, an endless row of vehicles—yellow taxis, Vespas, and impatient drivers—clogged the growing morning rush.

"Any alternative routes?" he asked, downshifting to first gear.

Sussie, engrossed in data on her iPad, squinted against the glare of the morning light reflecting off its screen. "Novus is sending real-time updates from surveillance cameras. Gavrail's team has split up—some heat signatures are moving toward the station, others are scattering across the city like a web." She paused, swiping through a fresh map. "Classic diversion tactics. They're trying to mask the real trail."

"How many in total?"

"Six distinct signatures. But with Gavrail... he's notorious for having backups we're not aware of."

A sudden, piercing bark forced Hugo to slam on the brakes. The car protested with a screech as an elderly woman in an elegant Burberry coat abruptly stopped in front of them. Her dachshund, a long-haired brown creature with a determined air, had slipped free from its handcrafted leather leash and was now zigzagging wildly between the cars.

"Scusi! Scusi! Napoleone, vieni qui!" the woman called desperately, clicking after the runaway dog in her Ferragamo heels.

"We're losing valuable time," Sussie checked her watch. "The Berlin train leaves in twenty-three minutes. If we miss it..." She left the sentence unfinished.

After what felt like an eternity, they finally broke free of the traffic jam, the engine's roar an echo of their shared frustration. But their progress was short-lived—orange traffic cones and barriers blocked the road less than four hundred meters from Termini Station.

"Parking garage there," Hugo pointed at an underground lot whose ramp glowed like an inviting cave. "We'll run the rest. Faster than finding another route."

They grabbed their tactical backpacks from the back seat—black Warrior Assault Systems packs compactly packed with everything from extra ammunition to medical supplies. The morning air hit them like a wall of heat as they sprinted into the street, their steps echoing against the ancient cobblestones, sweat already soaking through their clothes.

Roma Termini loomed ahead like a modernist cathedral of glass and steel, its façade a dramatic break from the city's classical architecture. Inside, they were met with a cacophony of sound and movement—digital speakers announcing departures in Italian and English, hard luggage wheels clattering on polished marble floors, and the hum of hundreds of conversations in dozens of languages blending into an incessant urban noise.

"Fredrika here," their discreet earpieces crackled to life.

"Confirmed visual on Gavrail's team. They've boarded ICE 993 to Berlin. Carriage 23. Two men in lab coats with a patient in a wheelchair. Tickets are waiting for you at kiosk four, code 47831."

Hugo swiftly keyed in the numbers on the kiosk's blinking screen. The tickets slid out with an electronic whirr, the paper still warm from the printer.

"Platform 7!" Sussie shouted over the station's din. "Three minutes to departure. We need to move now!"

They raced through the vast terminal, their trained bodies moving fluidly through the crowd. They weaved past confused groups of Japanese tourists with oversized cameras, Italian businessmen in immaculate suits, and backpackers lugging enormous packs.

A low, vibrating horn echoed through the station, its sound bouncing off the columns.

"Ultima chiamata, ICE 993 verso Berlino," a robotic voice announced over the loudspeakers, followed by the same message in German and English.

They leaped aboard the nearest door just as the departure whistle pierced the air. The train jolted and began to move as they stood panting in the narrow corridor, the air conditioning cool against their damp skin.

"We're onboard," Hugo reported quietly into his communicator as they started moving through the carriage. "Closing in on the target. Any visual on the exact position?"

Outside, Rome slid by in the morning haze, sunlight streaming through the station's massive glass roof in golden beams that made the dust in the air dance. But neither Hugo nor Sussie had time to admire the view. Somewhere on this train, just a few carriages away, was Dr. Rossi.

And Gavrail.

35

Outside Rome, Italy

The first-class compartment was surprisingly spacious, upholstered in deep blue velvet and polished Italian cherrywood that gleamed in the morning light. A low berth with crisp white Frette sheets was elegantly mounted along the right wall, while two foldable leather chairs in cognac-colored calfskin sat to the left. The air conditioning hummed discreetly as the train reached cruising speed, the Italian countryside streaking past outside in an impressionistic blend of terracotta buildings and olive-green hills. Rome receded behind them like a dream dissolving in the morning mist.

Dr. Rossi sat slumped in the chrome wheelchair, her head hanging so heavily forward that the bloodied bandage over her artificial eye nearly brushed her chest. Feverish beads of sweat sparkled like tiny diamonds on her forehead in the sunlight streaming through the compartment window. Her breathing was irregular but steady.

Gavrail and Nico occupied the two leather chairs, their postures relaxed but tinged with the ever-present vigilance of seasoned operatives. Gavrail's steely gray eyes reflected the passing landscape as he mentally reviewed the next phase, his fingers tapping a silent rhythm against the armrest.

He drew a deep, measured breath and nodded slowly. "Phase one executed within parameters. We've secured the Prometheus Eye and Dr. Rossi with the Genesis Eye." His voice was smooth as silk, but there was an undercurrent of steel in its tone. "This keeps us on track to complete the mission according to the Shadow Council's specifications."

Nico grinned, the scars on his weathered face pulling into a broad smile that made the knife marks shift like silver snakes across his cheek. "Fantastico, capo. I can't wait to see the Council's reward for this job." He rubbed his hands together eagerly. "This kind of tech... it's not just a goldmine; it's an entire diamond mine."

Gavrail nodded curtly. He hadn't earned his reputation as the industry's most efficient "problem solver" by counting rewards before the mission was complete. His path to this point had been one of precision and calculated violence—from his early years as an elite soldier in the French Foreign Legion to more... specialized assignments. Somehow, it had always seemed predestined that he would end up here, in this shadow world of secret contracts and high stakes.

Dr. Rossi suddenly stirred, a faint groan escaping her lips, catching their attention. Nico was instantly at her side, pulling out a discreet black medical bag and deftly drawing up a syringe filled with clear liquid.

"Just a little painkiller and adrenaline," he explained, administering the injection with the steady hand of a surgeon. "We need you awake for a little chat. Just some friendly conversation between colleagues."

Gradually, color returned to her pale cheeks. She blinked slowly with her uninjured eye, its pupil dilating as it focused on the men before her. The artificial eye beneath the bandage pulsed faintly, almost imperceptibly.

"Now then," Gavrail said softly, his tone almost paternal. "Tell us about the eye. How does the neural integration work? How does the digital overlay interact with the biological visual field?"

Dr. Rossi wet her dry lips with the tip of her tongue. "It... it's more than just a mechanical replacement." She swallowed hard. "The nanotechnology creates a direct neural link to the visual cortex. Biometric sensors and neuro-processors operate in perfect synchronization with the brain's natural signals..." She paused, as though each word caused her physical pain. "But without the proper activation sequence..."

"Go on," Nico prompted, his hand resting casually on the Beretta in his shoulder holster. "We've got plenty of time to go over the technical details."

A heavy silence fell over the compartment, broken only by the rhythmic clattering of the train on the rails. Gavrail rose silently, his movements as precise and fluid as a predator's.

"I need to make a call," he said neutrally, his face an unreadable mask. "Nico, keep an eye on our... guest. Ensure she remains... comfortable. She is to be delivered intact to our client."

He slipped into the corridor with soundless steps, closing the compartment door with an almost inaudible click. His hand found the encrypted satellite phone in his pocket. It was time to update Dr. Shinkelhof that they now had both the Prometheus Eye and Dr. Rossi.

For once, everything was proceeding as planned.

36

Berlin, Germany

Dr. Shinkelhof sank into his antique Chesterfield armchair with his characteristic poise, the burgundy leather creaking softly under his weight. His high-tech office on the fortieth floor of Shinkelhof Medical's headquarters usually offered a sweeping view of Berlin, but this morning, the city was cloaked in a layer of low-hanging clouds pressing against the reflective windows like gray cotton. The faint aroma of freshly brewed Blue Mountain coffee from his personal barista lingered in the room. Marius Witz, the company's Chief Financial Officer for the past twelve years, sat in the matching visitor's chair opposite him, a MacBook Pro open on the massive Italian walnut desk. His normally immaculate appearance—a portrait of German precision—showed clear signs of sleepless nights. His handmade Hermès tie was slightly askew, and his Egyptian cotton shirt had lost its crispness.

"The numbers... there's no way to sugarcoat this, Herr Doktor." Witz's voice was strained as he scrolled through the red figures on the screen. "Deutsche Bank has explicitly indicated they won't renew our credit facilities next quarter. Commerzbank is pulling out. Our debts now stand at 847 million euros, and with the escalating development costs of Project Prometheus..." He swallowed hard. "We barely have liquidity to cover next month's payroll."

"Marius," Shinkelhof interrupted, sipping his perfectly tempered espresso from a hand-painted Meissen cup, "how long have you been our Chief Financial Officer?"

"Twelve years, Herr Doktor. Since the merger with BioTech Munich."

"And in those twelve years," Shinkelhof set the cup carefully onto its matching saucer, "have I ever steered you, or this company, wrong? Have my decisions ever been... unsound?"

Witz adjusted his glasses nervously, a gesture betraying his rising anxiety. "No, of course not, but this situation is fundamentally differen—"

"Tomorrow," Shinkelhof rose in a fluid motion and approached the panoramic window spanning the entire wall, his perfectly tailored Brioni suit silhouetted sharply against the diffuse light, "we're holding a press conference at the Hotel Adlon Kempinski. Every major name in finance will be there—*Forbes*, *Financial Times*, *Der Spiegel*, *Wall Street Journal*." A small, almost predatory smile played at the corner of his lips. "And we have a... surprise for them. Something that will change everything."

"A surprise?" Witz frowned, his glasses sliding slightly down his nose. "Something that could salvage our catastrophic financial situation?"

Shinkelhof turned slowly, his movements deliberate and precise. "Let me ask you a question, Marius. A simple one: What would the market say about a product that not only revolutionizes medical technology but fundamentally changes the way humans interact with digital information?"

"Hypothetically..." Witz's fingers flew across the keyboard, performing rapid calculations. "With the right patents and aggressive marketing..."

"No, no, no." Shinkelhof waved his hand dismissively. "Think bigger. Much bigger. Imagine a technology that renders smartphones, tablets, computers—the entire current digital infrastructure—completely obsolete. A technology that gives the user direct neural access to all information, all data, in real time. That transforms the human being into a living digital interface."

Witz's hands froze over the keyboard. His eyes widened behind his glasses. "Herr Doktor... are you suggesting—"

"I'm not suggesting anything," Shinkelhof raised a hand imperiously. "I'm telling you that tomorrow's press conference will be... transformative. For the company. For the market." He paused dramatically, letting the words sink in. "For humanity."

"But the development costs of our projects have been astronomical. We've burned through reserves at an unprecedented rate, and none of them have—"

"All of it will seem like pocket change, like loose coins," Shinkelhof interrupted, "compared to the revenues that await us." He returned to his desk with purposeful strides, lifting an antique crystal decanter filled with century-old Rémy Martin Louis XIII. "What do your analysts say about the potential market for advanced neurological implants?"

"Rapidly growing," Witz replied, quickly consulting his projections. "Especially in the field of vision rehabilitation. The potential market value is estimated at over 50 billion euros annually by 2025."

"Multiply that by one hundred." Shinkelhof poured two fingers of the amber liquid into a hand-blown Baccarat glass with practiced precision. "When we reveal what we have... the entire market will explode."

"One hundred?" Witz's voice cracked. His trembling fingers punched numbers into the calculator. "That would mean... my God... five trillion?"

"Exactly." Shinkelhof extended one of the glasses with an elegant gesture. "And we will own it all—the patents, the technology, the implementation. Every... key to the kingdom, so to speak. Cheers, my dear Marius. To the future."

A charged silence hung in the air as Witz struggled to process the information. Outside, the clouds had begun to lift, and stray beams of sunlight pierced through, making Berlin's glass facades glimmer like diamonds.

"When will... the delivery arrive?" Witz finally asked, his voice cautious, as though walking a razor's edge.

Shinkelhof checked his Patek Philippe Grandmaster Chime—the world's most expensive wristwatch. "Very soon." A thin, knowing smile spread across his face. "Our... specialized consultants are the absolute best in the business. They have a flawless track record. They've never failed a mission."

His phone vibrated suddenly against the polished desk surface. The number was hidden, but Shinkelhof immediately recognized the distinctive format.

"Excuse me, Marius. I must take this call." He waited with impeccable courtesy until the CFO had closed the soundproofed door behind him before answering. "Yes?"

"We have the packages," said a smooth voice with a faint French accent. "But there are... complications requiring your immediate attention."

Shinkelhof's smile faded slowly, like frost melting under a morning sun, as he listened to Gavrail's report. Outside, Berlin continued to glimmer under the emerging sunlight, oblivious to the drama unfolding high above its streets.

37

Berlin, Germany

The icy knot in Shinkelhof's stomach tightened as he listened to Gavrail's voice through the encrypted line. His hand gripped the crystal glass of Louis XIII cognac so tightly that his knuckles turned white against the hand-blown glass. A single bead of sweat slid slowly down his temple, despite the perfectly regulated air in the office.

"You have them?" His voice was tense, controlled, but with an undercurrent of panic. "Where is Genesis? Where is Dr. Rossi?"

"Calm yourself. We have everything—Prometheus, Genesis, and Dr. Rossi."

Shinkelhof exhaled sharply, laughing in relief. "Wonderful!"

"But," Gavrail continued, his tone like a blade of ice, "we've received intel that we're being followed. By Novus."

Shinkelhof's smile vanished as his face turned ashen. He sank deeper into his Chesterfield armchair. "Novus?" The word escaped like a whispered curse. "I've heard Malaconda mention them. How much do they know? What are they—?"

"They know enough to deploy their top team," Gavrail interrupted. "Hugo Xavier and his operatives. Professionals. Ruthless. They're closing in on our position."

Shinkelhof stood abruptly and began pacing in front of the panoramic window. His reflection in the glass revealed a man on the brink of unraveling. "This is not good. Not good at all. Tomorrow, at eleven, I'm supposed to stand at the Adlon Kempinski and present this as the salvation of the company. Deutsche Bank, Commerzbank, *Financial Times*, *Forbes*—the entire financial elite will be there. I promised them a technological revolution that will change humanity. To succeed, I need all three components."

"Your corporate problems," Gavrail's voice was as cold as winter steel, "are irrelevant to me."

Shinkelhof clenched his fists so tightly that his nails bit into his palms. "The presentation... without a functioning demonstration..."

"With Novus chasing us across Europe?" Gavrail's tone dripped with sarcasm. "It complicates things significantly." A low, almost amused chuckle followed. "You're not just trying to save your crumbling empire, are you, Doctor?"

Shinkelhof felt cold sweat breaking out on his forehead. He discreetly wiped it away with a hand-woven silk handkerchief. "You're being paid to deliver results, Gavrail, not to ask questions about my business dealings."

"And you're desperate," Gavrail's voice was now smooth as wet velvet. "Desperate enough to schedule a world-changing presentation tomorrow without having all three necessary components secured. The question that nags at me is... what happens when the batteries run out? When Dr. Rossi vanishes with her secrets? When Novus..."

"There is no 'when,'" Shinkelhof forced out through gritted teeth, struggling to maintain composure. "You will deliver what you've been ordered to—Genesis, Prometheus, and Dr. Rossi— or certain... influential organizations will be extremely displeased. With both of us. And you know what that means."

A long, tense silence followed. The only sound was the faint hum of the air conditioning.

"Six hours," Gavrail said finally. "But the price has just doubled."

"Doubled?" Shinkelhof shot to his feet, his face flushing red with suppressed rage. "You can't change the terms in the middle of—"

"Already done," Gavrail interrupted, his tone almost paternal. "And Doctor? I won't ask again."

The line went dead with a sharp click. Shinkelhof stared at the silent phone in his trembling hand as the implications of the conversation sank in. Outside, Berlin continued its morning routine forty stories below, oblivious to the high-stakes drama playing out above its streets.

He turned to his high-definition screen and opened the presentation for tomorrow. The images of the revolutionary artificial eye—the innovation that was supposed to save his empire, secure his position in the Shadow Council, and change the world—now felt like a cruel joke without the delivery.

Six hours. Three hundred and sixty minutes. That was all that stood between triumph and total collapse. Between life and...

He drained the cognac in a single sweeping motion.

38

ICE 993 toward Berlin, somewhere in Europe

Hugo flexed his powerful back muscles and took a deep breath as he leaned against the compartment window, his tailored suit straining over a body coiled like a spring. The German countryside blurred past outside, a streak of motion in the train's high velocity, while the morning sun painted the horizon in shifting hues of gold and red. The rhythmic clatter of the train's wheels on the rails vibrated up through the floor, a steady beat in the tension-filled silence.

Sussie sat cross-legged on the dark blue berth, her fingers flying across a custom-modified Novus tablet with integrated neuroprocessors. The bluish glow from the screen lit her focused expression as lines of complex code scrolled rapidly across the display.

"The train's security system is... fascinatingly constructed," she murmured, her precise fingers continuing their work. "Deutsche Bahn has really stepped up their game since our last mission in Germany."

A sly, almost predatory smile curved her lips. "But, as usual, they overlooked a critical backdoor in the old analog framework. Amateurs."

"How much time do you need?" Hugo checked his watch, each lost minute slicing at him like a blade. "Dr. Rossi's condition was critical when they took her."

"Three, two, one..." Sussie's tablet pulsed softly with a blue glow as she breached the security system. "We're in. I'm accessing the corridor cameras now. Sixteen angles, full HD resolution."

Fredrika's sharp voice suddenly broke through their discreet earpieces. "Status?"

"Onboard and connected," Hugo reported, leaning over Sussie's shoulder to study the multiple camera feeds on the tablet. "No visual on the target yet. What's your situation?"

"Berlin police have been informed but are standing down per our instructions. Madeleine is coordinating directly with BND's counterterrorism unit." A tense pause. "Be extremely careful. Novus sent us a dossier on Gavrail, and his track record is... alarming. His last three missions resulted in a total of twenty-seven deaths. All 'accidents.'"

Sussie nodded gravely, methodically scrolling through different camera views. "We need to plant a direct microphone once we locate them. What about a standard RX-50 with directional pickup? Twenty-meter range through walls."

"Too risky," Hugo shook his head decisively. "Gavrail will be on high alert for electronic surveillance. He's old school—paranoid but thorough. We need something subtler."

"The QT-7, then." Sussie rummaged through her bag and produced what looked like an ordinary metal screw. "The latest from Novus's tech division. Looks like standard train hardware but contains a quantum audio sensor. Can be affixed to a doorframe as we pass. Battery life: forty-eight hours."

They continued monitoring the multiple camera feeds as the train thundered northward through the German countryside. The dining car began filling with early lunch patrons in business suits. A noisy family with small children bustled past in the corridor, the kids laughing and darting around. A conductor in a crisp uniform meticulously checked tickets in first class.

"There!" Sussie's finger froze mid-motion. On the screen, a tall man in a pristine white lab coat strode purposefully down the corridor of Car 23. His military-precise posture betrayed his otherwise casual facade.

Hugo leaned closer, his trained eye noting every detail. "Zoom in on his right hand and forearm."

Sussie manipulated the image with swift movements. A faint bulge under the lab coat's sleeve became visible—a professionally concealed holster, likely carrying a compact Beretta with a suppressor.

"That must be Nico," Sussie whispered intently. "Gavrail's right-hand man. He was with him during the Jakarta operation last year."

"Track him. Every move."

They watched in tense silence as the false doctor moved with feline precision down the corridor, pausing at compartment 2374. After a swift but thorough scan in both directions, he slipped silently through the door.

"Fredrika," Hugo's voice was low but brimming with intensity. "We have a probable location. Car 23, compartment 74. Confirmed presence of at least one of Gavrail's men."

"Understood." Fredrika's tone was steely. "Proceed with extreme caution. If Gavrail realizes you're monitoring... remember Bangkok."

"We do." Hugo turned to Sussie, his eyes dark with focus. "Time for some direct reconnaissance. I'll go first, scout the corridor. You follow with the QT-7 if I signal it's clear."

Sussie was already packing her advanced equipment into a discreet Prada shoulder bag that concealed its true contents. "And if it's not clear?"

Hugo checked his concealed SIG Sauer with a fluid, almost imperceptible motion. "Then we improvise. Like in Macau."

They exchanged a glance laden with years of shared experience, triumphs, and near disasters. After so many missions together, no further words were needed.

"Showtime," Sussie murmured as Hugo slid into the corridor, his movements relaxed yet carrying an undercurrent of coiled energy, his eyes scanning with sharp precision.

The hunt had reached its most critical phase. A single mistake now could not only cost Dr. Rossi her life but also place one of history's most revolutionary inventions into the hands of those who would use it to control rather than aid humanity.

39

ICE 993 toward Berlin, somewhere in Europe

The train corridor stretched ahead like a narrow, climate-controlled tunnel, barely a meter wide, with a low brushed-aluminum ceiling and dark blue compartment doors spaced at regular intervals on both sides. The morning light filtering through the tinted windows created shifting patterns of light and shadow as the ICE train swayed gently through the German countryside. The clink of Royal Copenhagen porcelain in first class, the aroma of freshly brewed Italian coffee, and the murmur of conversations in German, English, and French filled the confined air.

"I have visual on one near the dining car," Sussie reported quietly into her discreet communicator while pretending to scroll through her phone. "Wearing a Deutsche Bahn uniform, posing as serving staff. Another's covering the rear exit in Car 25, dressed as a train attendant. A third is moving between cars, civilian clothing but carrying a Heckler & Koch compact under his jacket."

"Tactically sound setup," Hugo murmured as he adjusted his tie in a mirrored wall, discreetly monitoring the corridor's reflection. "They're spread out in a classic diamond formation, controlling every possible escape and attack route. Also, we've received a file from the Italian police confirming the identity of a mercenary known as Gavrail."

A German family with two small children in navy coats struggled to maneuver their luggage through the narrow corridor. An elderly Italian woman in a Chanel suit cradling a white poodle waited impatiently to pass, her sharp perfume cutting through the train's sterile air. Every civilian passenger represented both a potential hostage and an innocent who could end up caught in the crossfire during a confrontation.

"Fredrika here," her voice crackled crisply in their earpieces. "I count five armed men strategically placed across three cars. Gavrail is staying within a constant three-meter radius of Dr. Rossi in Compartment 74. We also see... wait..." A brief pause. "Confirmed: medical equipment in the compartment. They're preparing something."

Hugo and Sussie approached the target compartment from opposite directions, their movements synchronized with the precision of years of joint operations. As a service cart loaded with Riedel crystal and Laurent-Perrier champagne passed by, it gave Sussie the perfect cover to surgically affix the QT-7 sensor—no larger than a fingernail—to the doorframe.

"Sensor active and linked," she confirmed, continuing past the compartment at a casual pace. "Signal clear and encrypted. Audio quality optimal."

"Immediate retreat," Fredrika instructed. "We're already receiving high-quality audio. First dialogue streaming in now." They returned to their compartment along separate, meticulously planned routes to avoid suspicion. Hugo passed through the dining car, ordering a double espresso with a flawless German accent to maintain his cover. Sussie made a strategic stop at the restroom, conducting a thorough electronic scan for hostile surveillance.

Back in their private compartment, Sussie activated her custom-built tablet with neuroprocessors. The feed from the QT-7 sensor streamed in with crystal-clear precision, undisturbed by the train's constant background noise.

"...time is running out faster than your patient's blood pressure," Gavrail's muffled voice came through, smooth as silk but laced with deadly intent. "Shinkelhof demands delivery within six hours. His patience, like his bank account, is running dry."

"You fundamentally misunderstand the situation. This isn't a negotiation about technical specifications. This is a deadline. And you are the package."

Hugo and Sussie exchanged a long look across the compartment table. The time pressure complicated an already volatile situation further.

"Update," Fredrika's sharp voice cut through the encrypted channel. "Berlin's central station has been notified and is prepared. GSG 9 special units are on standby at every scheduled stop. But be advised—civilian presence in the operational area means every intervention must be surgically precise. We cannot risk collateral damage."

The ICE train thundered northward through the German countryside, a hermetically sealed system of Swedish steel and German safety glass, as a deadly game of cat and mouse played out meter by meter. From Compartment 74, Dr. Rossi's and Gavrail's voices continued to stream through the hidden sensor, while Hugo and Sussie listened intently for every clue, every possible opening for an intervention.

Time ticked inexorably toward a confrontation none of them could avoid. The only question remaining was the price in blood it would demand.

40

ICE 993 toward Berlin, somewhere in Europe

Dr. Rossi's sweat-drenched forehead glistened under the dim LED lighting of the compartment, tiny droplets tracing paths down her pale face. Her breathing had grown more labored over the past hour. The improvised pressure bandage on her temple, made from a torn lab coat, was now soaked with fresh blood, its dark stain spreading ominously.

Gavrail stood at the window, his tall silhouette stark against the blur of the German landscape rushing past. His steel grip tightened around his encrypted phone as he listened to Shinkelhof's latest update. The controlled mask of his face betrayed faint but clear signs of mounting irritation—a tension around his eyes, a subtle twitch in his jaw.

"The patient's condition is deteriorating," Nico reported in a low, measured voice as he methodically checked Dr. Rossi's vitals. His fingertip pressed lightly against her wrist. "Blood pressure is dropping. Pulse irregular."

"Silence," Gavrail snapped, ending the call with a precise motion. He turned to Dr. Rossi, his gray eyes cold as winter steel. "You don't get to die yet, Doctor."

Dr. Rossi struggled to focus her good eye on him, her voice weak but still tinged with the authority of a seasoned scientist. "You... you don't understand."

In their compartment several cars away, Hugo and Sussie locked eyes, their expressions grim as they listened through the QT-7 sensor. Every word was transmitted with crystal clarity through their discreet earpieces.

"They're preparing something extensive," Sussie whispered, her fingers flying over her custom-built tablet with integrated neuroprocessors. "Significant activity in the compartment on thermal sensors. They're unpacking... wait..." She zoomed in on the readings. "Confirmed signature of surgical instruments. Metallic objects, sterile packaging."

A sudden jolt rippled through the entire train, followed by a noticeable deceleration that caused coffee cups in the dining car to clink. The ICE train's announcement system crackled to life with a digital chime:

"Meine Damen und Herren, wir haben eine technische Störung im Antriebssystem..."

"Technical issue in the propulsion system," Hugo translated swiftly. "The train is reducing speed for a safety diagnostic."

"Understood," Fredrika's voice was cold steel in their earpieces. "GSG 9's task force is still twenty minutes from the nearest station. You need to act immediately. Full authorization granted for direct action."

"We need an effective distraction," Sussie murmured, activating an advanced hacking program. Streams of code danced across her screen, the blue light reflecting in her determined eyes. "Give me thirty seconds with the train's electrical system. I'll isolate emergency lighting."

Hugo and Sussie exchanged a long look, the kind of wordless communication honed over years of shared missions. They had mere minutes to prevent disaster.

"Ready?" Hugo asked as he silently donned a lightweight bulletproof vest beneath his tailored jacket.

Sussie nodded sharply, her fingers poised over the tablet like a pianist before a crescendo. "On your signal. Three seconds from command to total blackout."

Outside, the train had slowed to a crawl, its wheels screeching in protest as the brakes engaged. The muted afternoon light filtering through the compartment windows began to fade as they approached a tunnel. Subtle surveillance was no longer an option. The real hunt was about to begin—and the stakes were no less than a woman's life and the fate of humanity's future.

41

ICE 993 toward Berlin, somewhere in Europe

Darkness fell like a hammer, absolute and disorienting. The sudden shift from dim afternoon light to total blackness struck with a near-physical force.

Sussie's precision hack had plunged the train corridor into a tunnel of impenetrable shadow. Panic erupted in multiple languages—German, English, Italian—as passengers stumbled and shouted in confusion. A baby's piercing wail cut through the chaos.

"Three, two..." Hugo counted under his breath, advancing with fluid precision. His silenced SIG Sauer was steady in a two-handed grip, his body moving effortlessly with the swaying train. At "one," the emergency exits in both directions burst open simultaneously, a coordinated diversion strategy. The sudden rush of air whipped loose papers and small items into a chaotic swirl.

From Compartment 74, Gavrail's sharp voice sliced through the uproar:

"Secure the patient! Nico, stop the procedure immediately! Marco, Pietro—corridor, now!"

The first shot cracked from the left—a suppressed *phut* that narrowly missed Hugo's head. He felt the heat of the bullet pass his ear and returned fire instinctively, two precise shots toward the muzzle flash. A string of colorful Italian curses followed, accompanied by the sound of a body diving for cover.

"Twelve civilians in active motion," Sussie reported through their comms, her fingers flying over her tablet as she monitored thermal readings. "Two German families in Car 22, an elderly Italian woman with a poodle in Car 23, businessmen in the dining car—"

"All passengers to the dining car, now!" Hugo barked in a commanding tone, his voice cutting through the chaos. "Schnell! Presto! Move!"

The emergency lights flickered on with a sputtering hum, casting eerie blue-white shadows along the corridor. Hugo spotted

Marco crouched behind an overturned service cart, shards of shattered Riedel crystal glittering at his feet. Pietro, moving with feline agility, was advancing toward the far end of the car. Classic crossfire tactics—they had done this before.

"Fredrika," Sussie's voice was tight with focus as she worked her tablet, streams of code reflected in her glasses. "The train is nearing Schönberg Tunnel. Two minutes until total blackout."

A sudden burst of automatic fire interrupted her. Pietro and Marco unleashed a coordinated assault, their H&K submachine guns roaring to life. Hugo dove behind a reinforced metal panel as glass exploded around him, raining shards like diamonds.

"They're stalling for time to evacuate," he muttered, methodically reloading as spent casings clinked against the floor. "Sussie?"

"Almost there... just one more firewall to bypass... got it!" she exclaimed. Instantly, the train's sprinkler system activated, unleashing a torrent of icy water.

In the chaos of water and movement, Hugo saw his opening. Rolling out from cover in a practiced maneuver, he fired twice. Both shots hit Marco in the thigh, dropping him with a muffled grunt. Pietro responded instantly, unleashing a volley that shredded the corridor wall where Hugo had been a split second before.

But it had only been a distraction.

The door to Compartment 74 slammed open, and Gavrail emerged, dragging Dr. Rossi with him as a human shield. A compact Beretta was pressed against her bloodied temple.

"So tragically predictable," Gavrail shouted over the cacophony, his voice cold and controlled despite the chaos. "Drop your weapons, or the doctor will demonstrate just how effective her cranial surgery can be. I assure you, my hand is far less steady than Nico's."

Hugo froze in his tactical position, cold water dripping down his neck as he assessed the situation. In his earpiece, Sussie's voice was a tense whisper:

"Tunnel in sixty seconds. Total blackout imminent."

Gavrail began backing toward the roof emergency hatch, dragging Dr. Rossi with calculated precision. "Nico, secure the surgical equipment. We'll take the more... scenic route."

That's when Hugo saw it—a subtle movement from Dr. Rossi. Her right hand, hidden from Gavrail's view by her own body, slowly formed three distinct signs: Left. Right. Duck.

The meaning was immediate and clear.

"Now!" Hugo shouted.

And chaos erupted. A symphony of movement, flashes of light, and deafening sound collided in an instant as hell broke loose.

42

ICE 993 toward Berlin, somewhere in Europe

The world erupted into chaos as Dr. Rossi threw herself to the left with a desperate burst of strength that caught both Gavrail and Hugo off guard. Her survival instincts drove her movements, her artificial eye faintly pulsing beneath the bloodied bandage. The sharp crack of shattering steel echoed through the train car as the emergency hatch was blown open by a precisely placed explosive charge—Nico's trademark handiwork. Cold air and the pungent scent of diesel rushed into the corridor, blending with the smoke and panic.

"Contact! Three armed tangos on the roof of Car 24!" Sussie's sharp voice cut through their encrypted comms.

Gavrail moved with the lethal precision of a predator. His grip on Dr. Rossi tightened like an iron vice as he backed toward the hatch, Prometheus's secure case slung over his shoulder. Pietro and Marco executed a flawless crossing maneuver, their movements choreographed to provide Gavrail cover. Every step was calculated, their coordination honed through years of combat.

"Hugo!"

Sussie's warning was drowned out by the deafening detonation of a flashbang grenade. The blinding burst of light reflected off the shattered glass of the corridor, creating a disorienting cascade of refracted brilliance.

Hugo dove instinctively to the side, feeling the searing heat of the explosion scorch his face. His trained reflexes fought to overcome the tinnitus-like ringing in his ears. Through the haze, he glimpsed Gavrail's elegant, almost balletic movements as he pulled Dr. Rossi through the hatch. Rain mingled with blood on her lab coat as she struggled against him.

"They're splitting up," Sussie said, her tone clipped as she analyzed real-time thermal feeds on her tablet. "Two distinct groups. Gavrail and Nico are evacuating with the target. Marco and Pietro are establishing a defensive position. Classic SEAL tactics."

Hugo calculated his next move while reloading his SIG Sauer with practiced efficiency. "Fredrika, update on GSG 9's position?"

"Still fifteen minutes from the intercept point," Fredrika's voice was tight with frustration. "Berlin's morning traffic is gridlocked. You're on your own."

A 9mm round ricocheted off the reinforced metal panel mere centimeters from Hugo's head, the energy vibrating through the air. Marco and Pietro pressed their advantage, using the lingering smoke from the flashbang as tactical cover.

"I'm going for high-ground engagement," Hugo decided, steeling himself for what lay ahead. "Sussie—"

"I'll neutralize the ground threats," she interrupted, drawing her custom-modified MP7 with a fluid motion. "Go! Now!"

Hugo surged forward, narrowly evading a burst of suppressive fire from Pietro. He grabbed the still-warm edge of the hatch, and with an explosive burst of strength born from countless hours of training, he pulled himself onto the roof.

The icy wind hit him like a wall, a howling tempest that turned every movement into a precarious dance on the knife-edge of disaster. The ICE train barreled forward at over 100 kilometers per hour, the landscape around them a blur of gray and green. Ahead, against the steel-gray horizon, Hugo saw Gavrail dragging the struggling Dr. Rossi across the slick surface while Nico guarded their flank with a compact automatic rifle.

"*Herr Xavier!*" Gavrail's voice carried effortlessly over the roaring wind, chillingly composed. "Is it truly worth the risk? At this speed, a single misstep is... fatal."

A deep, rumbling vibration reverberated through the train's structure. Hugo's eyes darted forward, and his professional calm cracked for a split second.

The tunnel.

They had less than 120 seconds before the train hurtled into the impenetrable darkness of the mountain pass. On the roof, there would be nowhere to go.

Below, the staccato of gunfire echoed as Sussie engaged Marco and Pietro in a precisely choreographed firefight. Above, the distant *wop-wop-wop* of rotor blades cut through the air—a helicopter closing in, likely a militarized Bell.

Time was bleeding away as fast as the blood seeping from Dr. Rossi's reopened wounds.

Hugo checked his SIG Sauer one final time and began moving forward with feline precision. Each step was a delicate balance between speed and the need for absolute footing.

The tunnel entrance loomed ahead, a gaping black maw ready to swallow them whole.

43

ICE 993 toward Berlin, somewhere in Europe

The tunnel loomed ahead with the unyielding inevitability of a well-orchestrated hell. The sleek roof of the ICE train vibrated beneath Hugo's custom tactical boots as he advanced with practiced precision. Each step was a calculated maneuver against the treacherously slick metal surface. Ahead of him, Gavrail and the struggling Dr. Rossi were silhouettes against the leaden sky, her resistance a stark contrast to his unshakable grip.

"Ninety seconds to tunnel!" Sussie's usually steady voice cracked with interference in his earpiece. Below, the relentless firefight continued, a chaotic symphony of gunfire, shattering glass, and panicked cries.

"It's over, Gavrail. Let her go," Hugo commanded, his voice cutting through the howling wind with the calm authority of experience. "You see the tunnel. You see the situation. There's no way out of this."

Gavrail turned partially toward him, a cold smile playing at his lips but never reaching his steely eyes. "On the contrary, Herr Xavier." He gave a subtle nod upward, and Hugo's gaze followed. The dark silhouette of the approaching helicopter grew larger against the muted winter sky.

Dr. Rossi twisted with renewed vigor, her movements frantic as the helicopter's powerful downdraft caused the entire train structure to sway alarmingly. Hugo seized the moment of instability, launching himself forward in a calculated strike.

Gavrail, his reflexes honed to a razor's edge, anticipated the move. He shoved Dr. Rossi to the side with brutal efficiency. She hit the slippery train roof with a muffled scream, rolling dangerously close to the edge.

What followed was a deadly dance of combat mastery.

The two men collided in an explosion of controlled violence. Hugo's right hook, perfectly timed, was met with Gavrail's parry, the force of their collision reverberating through the air. Every motion was a hair's breadth away from disaster, the roaring wind threatening to punish even the smallest misstep with certain death.

"Sixty seconds to tunnel!" Sussie's warning felt distant amid the growing static of the comms.

Nico, moving with his characteristic Sicilian agility, maneuvered toward Dr. Rossi, intent on reclaiming control. But she surprised them all by scrambling away with unexpected speed, dragging herself toward a safer position.

"This only ends one way," Gavrail muttered through gritted teeth as he delivered a precise elbow strike to Hugo's ribs, the blow carrying the weight of years of martial arts expertise. "One of us doesn't leave this roof alive."

Hugo absorbed the pain, countering with a flawless shoulder throw that nearly unbalanced the legendary assassin. "Agreed. With you in cuffs and the technology secured."

The tunnel's gaping mouth was so close now that its oppressive darkness seemed to reach out toward them, a physical force rushing to swallow them whole. Above, the Bell helicopter hovered perilously low, its rotor wash transforming the falling rain into a blinding mist.

In a split second, Hugo saw his opening.

Dr. Rossi, edging closer to the center of the train roof, reached into her lab coat with trembling fingers. The faint glint of metal caught Hugo's eye—she had managed to retrieve a scalpel, her hand steady despite her weakened state. She glanced at Hugo, her expression a mix of fear and determination, and nodded.

Hugo lunged forward with ferocious speed, his movement synchronized with Rossi's sudden lunge at Gavrail's legs. The assassin's balance faltered as he instinctively shifted to counter her attack.

"Now!" Hugo roared, driving all his weight into a final strike. The world erupted into chaos.

44

ICE 993 toward Berlin, somewhere in Europe

In the blinding chaos, Hugo seized his chance, launching himself toward Gavrail with explosive force. At the same time, the train's automatic warning system blared through the speakers—collision with the tunnel's walls was now mere seconds away.
"Now!" Gavrail's command cut through the roaring wind with military precision.
The matte-black Bell helicopter swooped down to an almost impossible height over the speeding train. From its belly, a Kevlar-reinforced tactical line descended, equipped with a quick-release harness swaying in the turbulent air. Gavrail, with movements betraying years of elite training, gripped the harness with one hand while delivering a surgically precise kick to Hugo's solar plexus with the other.
"Prometheus is secured!" Nico shouted triumphantly, holding up the gleaming prototype in its specialized transport case. He hooked his own harness onto a second line, his movements as efficient and practiced as his commander's.
Hugo, gasping from the impact, clawed his way back to his knees on the slippery train roof. Dr. Rossi was crawling toward him, blood streaking her face and soaking into her torn lab coat.
"Thirty seconds to tunnel!" Sussie's voice was tight with barely contained panic in his comms. "Hugo, you need to evacuate the roof immediately! Collision imminent!"
The tunnel's yawning black maw loomed ahead, an unforgiving monument of concrete rushing toward them like the jaws of a prehistoric beast. Above, the helicopter began to ascend, pulling Gavrail and Nico off the train roof in a perfectly timed arc. Cold rain lashed their faces as the ICE train barreled toward its unavoidable rendezvous with the tunnel.
"Hold on! Now!" Hugo grabbed Dr. Rossi around the waist, hurling both of them through the emergency hatch in a

calculated, controlled fall. They tumbled into the corridor below in a tight roll just as the concrete roof of the tunnel scraped past above, mere centimeters from Hugo's hair.

The impact rattled through them as they hit the corridor floor, rolling to disperse the force of the fall. Around them lay the chaotic aftermath of the firefight—shattered safety glass glittered like diamonds in the emergency lighting, spent 9mm shell casings clinked as they rolled across the floor, and a faint haze of tear gas hung in the air like a ghostly veil.

Sussie was there to meet them, her MP7 still trained with steady hands, her eyes scanning for lingering threats.

"Marco and Pietro?" Hugo asked, checking Dr. Rossi's vitals with practiced hands. Her pulse was weak but steady.

"Neutralized with non-lethal force. Securely restrained," Sussie replied, her voice crisp with professionalism. She activated her communicator. "Fredrika, primary target secured. Dr. Rossi is safe. But…" She hesitated, exchanging a glance with Hugo.

"They have Prometheus," Hugo finished bitterly, wiping a mix of blood and rain from his face. His gaze drifted toward the shattered window, through which the black helicopter was now a shrinking speck against the brooding winter sky. "They have the advanced prototype."

Dr. Rossi suddenly grabbed his arm with surprising strength, her fingers digging into his skin like steel clamps. "But how much battery is left?" she rasped, her eyes sharp despite her injuries.

The train roared through the tunnel, its vibrations a relentless reminder of the narrow escape. Outside, the rising wail of GSG 9's sirens grew louder, signaling the arrival of reinforcements.

One battle was won—Dr. Rossi was safe. But as Hugo stared toward the distant horizon where the helicopter had vanished, he knew this was only the beginning.

Shinkelhof and the Shadow Council had revealed their true faces.

The war had just begun.

45

ICE 993 toward Berlin, somewhere in Europe

The black Bell 412 helicopter ascended through the early morning mist, its matte fuselage blending seamlessly with the dim gray of the predawn sky. Gavrail sat in the co-pilot's seat, his ice-gray eyes fixed on the high-tech cryogenic container resting on his lap. The Prometheus prototype, suspended in a bath of shimmering blue coolant, gleamed faintly in the shifting light of the instrument panel.

Beside him, Nico worked methodically, staunching the bleeding from the gunshot wound in his shoulder. His experienced hands moved with precision as he applied an advanced coagulant powder, his expression set in grim determination.

"Status on the unit?" Gavrail's voice cut through the helicopter's intercom with icy precision. "Show me the diagnostics."

"Biometric readings stable," Nico replied, glancing at the holographic display projected from his custom tablet. Beads of sweat glistened on his forehead, betraying the pain he was suppressing. "Temperature: minus five degrees Celsius. Neural activity within acceptable parameters. But..." He frowned, pulling up a complex waveform on the screen. "The battery's down to its last twenty percent. How did it drain so quickly?" He adjusted the tablet, his brow furrowing deeper. "There's something... off about the signature pattern. Like an echo we can't account for."

Gavrail's jaw tightened slightly as he activated his quantum-secured satellite phone with a practiced motion. "Dr. Shinkelhof. Update: the package is secure. ETA Berlin: four hours." His tone was clipped, efficient.

He listened intently for a moment, his steely demeanor unshaken, though his grip on the phone was rigid. "Understood. Hotel Adlon, 0900 tomorrow. Preparations?" Another brief pause. "No compromises on security. But we've lost Dr. Rossi."

*

A few hours later, at a local hospital somewhere between Italy and Germany, Hugo coordinated the urgent evacuation as chaotic scenes unfolded in the hallways. Sussie stood guard at the door, her compact MP7 concealed under a "borrowed" doctor's coat.

Dr. Rossi rose from the hospital bed with a vigor that surprised them both.

"My injuries are mostly superficial," she explained while efficiently disconnecting the monitoring equipment. "I feigned weakness to fool Gavrail. He thinks I'm too frail to escape."

Hugo raised an impressed eyebrow. "Smart tactic. The helicopter is waiting on the roof."

Hugo's phone vibrated: Fredrika.

"Shinkelhof just booked the entire top floor of Hotel Adlon," she reported, the sound of typing echoing in the background. "Press conference tomorrow at 0900. Reuters, Bloomberg, Financial Times—every major player in the financial world will be there."

A couple of hours later, they packed up and headed upward. They reached the roof, where a sleek black Bell 429 awaited, its rotors spinning. Dr. Rossi climbed in with practiced ease, followed by Hugo and Sussie.

"Call Madeleine, Fredrika," Hugo ordered as the helicopter lifted off. "We need a fully operational team in Berlin. Set up a cover for the press conference. And Fredrika..." he paused as the city stretched out below them, "contact our German contacts. This is going to get complicated."

Fredrika gave a thumbs-up. Dr. Rossi shook her head as she examined technical data on her tablet. "Reinhart has always been obsessed with power. Back at university in Munich..." She paused, a bitter smile playing across her lips. "We were research partners once, can you believe that? Brilliant young scientists who were going to change the world."

"What happened?" Sussie asked while securing the door.

"We developed the first prototypes together. But our visions diverged. I saw the potential to help people regain their sight. Reinhart..." She hesitated. "He only saw profit and control. When I refused to commercialize the technology on his terms, he stole half of the research data and started Shinkelhof Medical."

"And now he has Prometheus," Hugo remarked.

"Yes, but he doesn't understand its full potential—or its dangers. Without power, it'll die when the battery runs out. And it requires a very specific power source to keep the battery charged. That technology only BioVita possesses." Dr. Rossi touched the bandage unconsciously.

"Five hours' flight to Berlin," she said, reviewing more data on her tablet. "We have a lot to prepare. Prometheus is more powerful than any of you realize, and Reinhart has no idea what he's unleashing."

"You mentioned you worked together?" Sussie prompted.

Dr. Rossi nodded, her gaze distant. "University of Munich. We were young, brilliant, convinced we could change the world. The first prototypes were catastrophic failures—conventional processors were far too slow to handle the enormous volume of visual data the brain processes."

She swiped at her tablet, projecting a holographic diagram into the air between them. "Then we made our first major breakthrough—the brain doesn't process visual information linearly. It uses quantum-mechanical patterns, superimposed states. That was the key to everything."

"Neuroprocessors?" Hugo asked. "Like quantum computers?"

"Far more sophisticated." Dr. Rossi manipulated the hologram, displaying a complex matrix of interacting quantum fields. "We developed biomimetic neuroprocessors capable of mimicking the brain's natural quantum-mechanical processes. *Genesis* was the first successful implementation." She touched the bandage again. "A perfect synthesis of biological tissue and quantum mechanics."

"But something went wrong," Sussie concluded.

"Reinhart became obsessed. He saw potential for something far darker than restoring vision." Dr. Rossi deactivated the hologram with a sharp gesture. "Prometheus includes a modified neuroprocessor designed not only to process but also to manipulate neural signals. A system capable of monitoring, controlling, and even rewriting neural patterns."

"Which is why the Shadow Council is interested," Hugo said.

"Exactly. Imagine—millions of people with Prometheus implants. Every visual input, every memory, every thought... all processed through quantum matrices that can be controlled remotely." Dr. Rossi leaned forward, looking out the window at the rising sun. "Reinhart thinks he can control the power he's unleashed. That's always been his greatest weakness—wanting to control the uncontrollable."

The helicopter turned eastward toward Berlin as the sun rose over the horizon.

46

Hotel Adlon Kempinski Berlin, Germany

The massive crystal chandeliers in Hotel Adlon's grand conference hall hung like frozen waterfalls from the ceiling, their golden glow casting a web of shadows over rows of handcrafted mahogany chairs. Midnight had long passed, and the oppressive silence was broken only by the hollow whispers of the ventilation system and Dr. Shinkelhof's feverish footsteps across the handwoven Persian rug, its intricate patterns seeming to dance in the flickering light.

"No, no, no, this is completely unacceptable!" His voice trembled with suppressed panic as he gestured wildly at the two technicians meticulously adjusting the advanced control panel. His Brioni suit, normally a masterpiece of Italian tailoring, was now rumpled and sweat-soaked after hours of manic effort. The air in the room felt electric, charged with an almost palpable desperation. "Prometheus demands precisely balanced power. Precisely!"

"Sir," Dr. Zhang leaned over the holographic display, her face ghostly in the pulsating blue glow of the meters. "The battery level is dropping faster than anticipated. Much faster."

"I know!" Shinkelhof gripped the podium so tightly that his knuckles turned white as bone. His bloodshot eyes bore the marks of sleeplessness and stress. "Do you think I don't know? We need Dr. Rossi. Without her..." He swallowed hard. "Without her, we can't restore the power supply properly."

Dr. Weber, a young technician whose hands shook slightly from both exhaustion and nerves, gingerly adjusted a control while beads of sweat glistened on his brow. "We're trying to compensate with external power, but the biological components are reacting negatively. It's like trying to tame a living organism actively resisting us. Without Dr. Rossi's calibration protocols, we risk permanent damage to—"

"Show me the diagnostics again," Shinkelhof interrupted, his eyes fixed on the dying prototype. Once vibrant with a clear blue glow, it now flickered weakly, irregularly—like a failing heartbeat. "There must be something we've missed. Some way around the security systems."

Dr. Zhang projected a complex holographic model of the prototype's internal systems. Red warning markers blinked like wounded stars across nearly every component, and the sound of the diagnostic system's alerts filled the room with a cacophony of beeps and buzzes.

"As you can see, the situation is far more critical than we initially assumed," she explained, zooming in on the energy diagnostics with hands that trembled almost imperceptibly. "Without Dr. Rossi's expertise, we can't even begin to understand how to recalibrate—"

"Dr. Shinkelhof?" A security guard in a discreet black suit materialized silently in the doorway. His face was a mask of professional neutrality. "The first journalists have started arriving. The Financial Times team is already waiting in the lobby."

Shinkelhof felt the panic in his chest intensify, a cold maelstrom threatening to engulf him. Soon, he would stand on this stage before the world's leading tech journalists and investors, presenting the technology meant to save his empire from the brink of ruin. But without Dr. Rossi...

"More stimulants," he ordered, his voice cracking under the strain of exhaustion and despair. "And call Gavrail again. He *must* find her. He *must* get her, and Genesis. Otherwise..." His voice trailed off as he stared out through the tall windows at Berlin's lights, shimmering coldly like indifferent stars. "Otherwise, it's all over."

47

Hotel Adlon Kempinski Berlin, Germany

By two in the morning, Dr. Shinkelhof finally retreated to the presidential suite on Hotel Adlon's top floor. The lights of Berlin glittered like jewels beyond the immense panoramic windows, with the Brandenburg Gate majestically illuminated in the distance. His reflection in the glass showed a man on the brink of collapse—suit crumpled, tie loosened, eyes bloodshot from exhaustion and stress.

With trembling hands, he poured a generous measure of Louis XIII cognac into a hand-blown Baccarat glass. The amber liquid caught the glow of the chandelier as he activated the quantum-secured communications device hidden within an antique walnut desk.

"Alexandria Protocol activated," announced the synthetic voice with its distinctive metallic echo. "Encryption maximum. Quantum link established."

Malaconda's holographic avatar materialized in the room's dim lighting, projected with such realism it seemed the Shadow Council's leader was physically present. His bespoke Brioni suit and perfectly groomed silver hair couldn't disguise the predatory sharpness in his gaze. Even as a hologram, he exuded authority, prompting Shinkelhof to unconsciously straighten his posture.

"The situation has... complicated," began Malaconda, his voice smooth like aged cognac but with an undertone of cold steel. "Our intelligence has just confirmed that Novus operatives landed at Tegel Airport forty-five minutes ago. Under false identities, of course, but our sources are certain."

Shinkelhof swallowed hard, feeling sweat bead on his forehead.

"And they were the ones who fought Gavrail on the train?"

Malaconda took a few holographic steps closer, his eyes piercing through Shinkelhof. "Hugo Xavier and his team are closing in."

"But Gavrail…" Shinkelhof tightened his grip on the cognac glass, his knuckles turning white. "He assured me that security—"

"Security?" A cold laugh sent a shiver down his spine. "Do you think that will stop anyone from Novus?" Malaconda shook his head slightly. "No, my dear doctor, we need… alternative arrangements."

"What do you suggest?" Shinkelhof's voice was barely above a whisper.

"First, we need insurance." Malaconda's holographic hand made an elegant gesture. "Dr. Rossi was more… creative with her security protocols than we anticipated. If tomorrow's demonstration fails, we need a backup plan."

"But the stock market… the investors…"

"If there's the slightest problem," Malaconda's voice dropped to an almost hypnotic whisper, "we'll activate Protocol Omega. I've already positioned assets capable of… managing the situation."

A heavy silence fell over the room as Malaconda outlined his plan in chilling detail. When the hologram finally faded, Shinkelhof had drained his third glass of cognac. The city outside seemed darker than ever, its lights now more threatening than inviting.

His hand trembled as he picked up his phone to contact Gavrail. On the desk before him, the encrypted communications device still pulsed with a faint blue glow, eerily reminiscent of the artificial eye that would decide his fate in less than seven hours.

"Dr. Shinkelhof?" A tentative knock at the door—it was Weber again. "The technicians need your approval for the final adjustments to the podium."

Shinkelhof adjusted his tie, trying to steady himself. But his hands wouldn't stop shaking.

48

Berlin, Germany

Forty meters beneath Berlin's bustling streets lay an abandoned subway station from the Cold War era. The vaulted walls of exposed brick and steel spoke of another time, but the cutting-edge technology filling the room was distinctly 21st century. Madeleine had called in a favor, and Hugo and his team had secured access to the old station. Holographic displays cast an eerie blue glow over the massive walnut conference table where the team had gathered. The air buzzed with the hum of electronics and mounting tension.

"Hotel Adlon," Sussie said, elegantly swiping her hands through the air to summon a three-dimensional blueprint. Her eyes reflected the blue light of the holograms as she zoomed in on key details. "Originally built in 1907, completely destroyed during World War II, rebuilt and renovated in 1997. Seven floors, two underground levels, a total of 382 rooms. Shinkelhof hasn't just booked the top floor—he's commandeered the entire security system."

"Show me the security protocols," Hugo leaned forward, his intense gaze locked on the rotating projection. His scarred knuckles rested on the table as he scrutinized the marked entry points.

"You're not going to like this," Sussie warned as she manipulated the display again. Red points began to flash across the model. "State-of-the-art Kroll system. Biometric locks with triple authentication, infrared heat sensors in every corridor, motion detectors with AI-based recognition." Her fingers danced through the air, highlighting critical security nodes with glowing markers. "But, as always, every system has a weakness—especially when you know exactly where to look."

Fredrika's voice cut through the communications system from London, crystal clear despite the distance. "Update from our sources in Berlin. Gavrail has positioned at least twelve men strategically throughout the building. All elite-trained, likely ex-military or special forces. And..." she paused significantly, "we've just confirmed that Malaconda himself is on his way to Berlin. His private jet took off from Paris twenty minutes ago."

"The window of opportunity is narrowing," Madeleine noted from her position at the end of the table. Despite the pain from her injuries, she sat upright, her authority undiminished. "The press conference starts at exactly 0900. We need to be in position before Shinkelhof unveils Prometheus."

"What do our analyses say about the guest profile?" Hugo asked, reviewing the guest list scrolling past in midair.

"One hundred invited guests," Sussie replied. "Primarily financial elites—bank directors, stockbrokers, tech investors. Plus fifty accredited journalists from the world's leading financial media. It's going to be packed."

"Which gives us both cover and complications," Hugo muttered. "More civilians mean more chaos to hide in, but also more potential casualties if something goes wrong."

"We have an advantage they won't expect," Madeleine leaned forward, her voice sharp with determination. "Dr. Rossi. She doesn't just know the system—she built it. Every security protocol, every backup routine..."

"And every weakness," Hugo finished. He stood slowly, his shadow stretching long against the brick wall. "We get one chance. Just one. If Shinkelhof unveils Prometheus to the world press as their own invention..." He let the sentence trail off.

"He won't," Sussie said, her voice steely as she downloaded the final security protocols to her custom-built tablet. "Not as long as I have anything to say about it."

In the subterranean room, the tension was almost palpable as they fine-tuned every detail of what would be the most dangerous operation in Novus's history.

Outside, on Berlin's streets, the city was beginning to awaken, unaware of the drama about to unfold in its historic heart.

"There's a lot at stake," Madeleine's voice sliced through the concentrated silence.

Hugo nodded gravely, performing a final check of his gear. Six hours to the press conference. Six hours.

49

Berlin, Germany

Hugo withdrew to a small control room adjacent to the main operations center, a high-tech cocoon housed within the concrete walls of the old tunnel system. Dozens of holographic screens floated in the air around him, each displaying real-time surveillance feeds from Hotel Adlon. The subdued lighting and the constant hum of servers created an almost otherworldly atmosphere.

Fredrika's avatar materialized in front of him in life-size detail, so lifelike that he could almost see the tension in her jaw. Her usually composed, professional demeanor was marred by something rare—genuine concern.

"The Shadow Council is mobilizing resources on a scale we've never seen before," she reported as intricate data patterns scrolled through the air between them. "Look at this—bank transfers through thirteen separate shadow accounts, movements across four continents, political connections activated at the highest levels in three governments. Hugo..." she hesitated, "everything points to this being far bigger than just Shinkelhof Medical and a stolen prototype."

"Pull up the communication logs from Rome again," Hugo requested, massaging his temple where a scar from the Berlin operation was still healing. He studied the intricate web of encrypted messages flickering past. "There—see? 0347, six hours before we even hit the hospital. Someone tipped them off. Someone knew exactly when we were going to strike."

"That means the leak must be someone with top-level clearance," Fredrika said, her voice strained. "Someone with direct access to our highest security protocols. Someone who knows Madeleine's inner circle, operational protocols, even the rotation schedules."

A red warning light suddenly began pulsing on one of the peripheral screens—unexpected movement at the hotel's western service entrance. They watched in tense silence as Gavrail arrived in an armored Mercedes S-Class, flanked by two discreetly armed men.

"Damn," Hugo muttered. "He's several hours earlier than intelligence predicted. Someone tipped him off about our surveillance."

"Hugo…" Fredrika's holographic hand moved as if to rest on his shoulder. She paused, choosing her words carefully. "If we're wrong about the traitor… if we're trusting the wrong person right now…"

"Then we're all dead before the sun rises over Berlin," he finished grimly. His eyes flicked back to the security feeds, tracking how Gavrail's men methodically took positions around the hotel. "And the world will wake up to a new order governed by the Shadow Council's technology."

A heavy silence fell between them, broken only by the muted hum of equipment. On one of the screens, they could see Dr. Rossi resting in a secure room two floors up.

"There's one more thing," Fredrika said at last. "Something that worries me even more than the traitor." She brought up a new data series. "These energy readings from the Prometheus prototype… they don't match our previous scans. It's as if…"

"As if what?"

"As if it's evolving. Changing. Growing." She shook her head, the worry etched deep into her expression. "And if that's true, if the prototype really is self-learning at this level…"

"Then we have far bigger problems than a traitor," Hugo said, his tone sharp as he activated his comm link to the team.

It was time to put the plan into motion.

50

Malmoe, Sweden

Madeleine Singh stood at the tall panoramic window of her private office at Novus headquarters. The darkness was beginning to yield to a leaden dawn over the Öresund, and the first fishing boats appeared as solitary pinpricks of light on the glassy water. She suppressed a grimace as she carefully adjusted her stance—the wound in her side from the recent attack still burned with an intensity that brought sweat to her brow. The doctors had insisted on at least two more weeks of rest. But rest was a luxury she could not afford now.

She and Fredrika had spent the night debriefing with Mikko and Freya, reviewing the extraordinary events of the past 24 hours. While some matters would have to wait, Berlin was the immediate priority.

"Show me Berlin again," she commanded the holographic display, her voice steady despite the pain. A detailed 3D map of the operational zone around Hotel Adlon materialized before her. Small blue lights indicated her agents' positions, while red markers displayed Gavrail's known security personnel. Too many red points, she thought. Far too organized.

A soft beep from her quantum computer drew her attention. The specialized encryption algorithm she had been running on their internal communications had finally yielded results. As she scrolled through the data, it felt as though the ground disappeared beneath her feet.

"This is impossible," she whispered, her eyes scanning the intricate communication patterns. "It can't... no one at that level would..." She paused as a particular sequence caught her attention. "Oh, God. That's why..."

A discreet knock on the polished rosewood door interrupted her thoughts. "Come in."

Fredrika entered, her expression grim.

"We have a critical situation in Berlin. Gavrail arrived at the hotel ten minutes ago. Three hours earlier than our intelligence predicted."

"Of course he did," Madeleine replied bitterly, projecting a series of encrypted messages into the air between them. The complex code sequences reflected in her tired eyes. "Because someone told him exactly when and where we'd be watching the hotel. Look here—these communication patterns."
"Should we abort the operation?"
"No." Madeleine's voice regained its steely edge. "We cannot let Shinkelhof unveil Prometheus to the world press. Whatever the cost, we have to stop him." She rose slowly, refusing to let the pain show. "But we'll do it my way."
"Which is?"
A faint smile crossed Madeleine's lips. "It's time to play the traitor's hand. Let them think they know our plan. Meanwhile..." She projected a new set of commands. "Activate Protocol Midnight."
Fredrika's eyes widened as she saw the codes. "That protocol has never been tested in the field. The risks—"
"Are less than the risks of failure," Madeleine interrupted, turning back to the window. The sun was now cresting the horizon, painting the sky in shades of blood and gold. "Contact Hugo. Tell him the plan has changed."
Fredrika nodded and left, leaving Madeleine alone with the weight of her decision. Somewhere in Berlin, Novus's best operatives were preparing for yet another life-threatening mission.
She touched the wound in her side, feeling the bandages beneath her tailored blouse. A reminder of the price of trust. A price she would not pay again.

51

Berlin, Germany

The morning sun gilded Hotel Adlon's imposing façade as the first journalists began arriving through its grand revolving doors. In the background, the Brandenburg Gate loomed majestically against the crisp blue October sky, its historic silhouette casting long shadows over the polished granite steps of the hotel.

Gavrail stood discreetly by the marble-clad reception desk, his tactical vest and silenced Sig Sauer elegantly concealed beneath a tailored Tom Ford suit that carried the faint scent of exclusive aftershave.

"Mr. Weber," Gavrail addressed the hotel's head of security, a gray-haired man in a sharply pressed uniform. "Are all security cameras calibrated to the specifications?"

Weber nodded, scrolling through his digital schedule on a tablet. The soft tapping of his fingers on the screen blended with the hum of conversation in the lobby. "Yes, and our guards have been briefed on your protocols. We've reinforced surveillance at all entrances, particularly the service doors at the rear."

The sound of heels clicking against the marble floor echoed through the lofty lobby as Sarah Chen of *Financial Times* entered through the revolving doors. Her Bottega Veneta laptop bag hung heavily at her side—too heavy to carry just a computer. The subtle trail of her expensive perfume lingered as she walked past.

"Possible competitor," Gavrail murmured into his concealed microphone, his voice barely audible. "Sector A. Keep an eye on her."

Weber frowned and leaned closer. "Shall we search the bag?"

"Not yet," Gavrail replied, observing Chen's movements through the lobby. "We don't want to draw attention. Let her feel secure."

The gilded crystal chandelier above cast a warm glow over the antique mahogany-paneled room as more journalists streamed in. The aroma of freshly brewed coffee from the hotel's award-winning café mingled with the light citrus scent of fresh floral arrangements adorning each table.

"*Financial Times* team is in place," reported a security guard through Gavrail's earpiece. "*Wall Street Journal* arriving in five minutes."

Weber checked his tablet again. "The conference hall is prepared to your specifications. Additional security personnel are stationed at all emergency exits, and we've secured the ventilation system."

Gavrail nodded in approval. The professionalism of the hotel staff was impressive—exactly what was needed for an operation of this magnitude.

Time marched inexorably forward as Hotel Adlon's elegant lobby filled with the world's financial elite. They mingled casually among the antique pillars and gilded mirrors, blissfully unaware of the tension simmering beneath the surface. The scent of exclusive perfumes, freshly pressed linens, and polished wood created an atmosphere of luxury and privilege—a perfect façade for the events about to unfold.

52

Berlin, Germany

The time was just past 3 a.m. in the presidential suite of Hotel Adlon. Dr. Shinkelhof stood before the vast wall of windows, gazing out as Berlin sprawled beneath him like an endless sea of pulsating lights. In the distance, the Brandenburg Gate stood illuminated, a ghostly monument to history. His reflection in the misted glass revealed a man teetering on the edge of collapse— his Egyptian cotton shirt hopelessly wrinkled, his Hermès tie hanging loose around his neck, and his bloodshot eyes a testament to sleepless nights and an increasing dependence on stimulants.

"Start over," he muttered, turning to the advanced holographic projection of Prometheus that rotated slowly in the air before him. The display flickered ominously, the battery level now critically low. "Increase power by twenty percent."

"Sir," Dr. Zhang interjected, shaking her head as she studied the pulsing monitors. The bluish glow of the control panel cast eerie shadows over her face. "We've already overloaded the external power supply three times. The system can't handle any additional load. Every attempt to force more power only accelerates the collapse."

"She's right," agreed Dr. Weber, his eyes fixed on the neural patterns displayed on his screen. His fingers danced frantically across the keyboard with desperate precision. "Look here—the synaptic connections are breaking down exponentially. It's as if... as if Prometheus is actively rejecting our attempts to stabilize it."

Shinkelhof gripped the edge of the console so tightly his knuckles turned white. On the holographic display, Prometheus emitted a steadily weakening blue glow. Indicators for critical systems blinked red across the control panel, their warning tones echoing through the room like the tolling of a death knell.

"Doctor?" His assistant appeared hesitantly in the doorway, carrying a new silver tray with espresso and an assortment of pastries none of them would touch. The pale fluorescent light from the corridor cast long shadows across his anxious face. The aroma of freshly brewed coffee mingled with the sterile scent of overheated electronics. "The security team reports increased activity in the hotel area. And the Tokyo Stock Exchange just opened—our shares are down another eight percent in pre-market trading..."

"Out!" Shinkelhof's voice lashed through the room like a whip. Grabbing an empty espresso cup, he hurled it against the wall, where it shattered in a cascade of porcelain shards. The sound echoed through the suite. "No one disturbs me! No one! Not until..." His voice faltered. "Not until we make the system work."

"Sir," Dr. Zhang spoke cautiously, as though addressing a wounded animal. "The system is too unstable. The neural networks are collapsing faster than we can repair them." She paused as a new alert blinked on the screen, its red glow reflected in her glasses.

"Batteries are down to eight percent," Dr. Weber reported tensely, his trembling fingers hovering over the keyboard. "The biological components are showing signs of permanent degradation. We need to shut it down before—"

Shinkelhof slumped into one of the suite's antique armchairs. The leather creaked under his weight as his hands trembled uncontrollably. On the massive walnut desk before him lay the company's latest stock figures, scattered like silent accusations—graphs and charts all plunging downward like condemning fingers.

"I was so close," he whispered, staring at the dying prototype. His voice quavered with exhaustion and despair. "Prometheus was going to revolutionize everything... change the world..." His bitter laugh echoed hollowly through the room.

"Batteries down to six percent," Dr. Zhang reported flatly. The faint scent of burning electronics began to fill the air. "Neural networks collapsing..." She trailed off as another warning light began to flash, its piercing alarm cutting through the air.

"Soon," Shinkelhof murmured to the dying prototype, his voice barely audible over the blaring alarms. "Soon everything will change. The world will understand... they *must* understand..."

53

Paris, France

The medieval chamber stretched like a dark crypt forty meters beneath the historic streets of Paris, a place whose existence was a closely guarded secret known only to a handful of the world's most powerful individuals. Antique crystal chandeliers, looted from the Russian Imperial Court during the chaos of the revolution, cast a muted, almost ghostly golden glow over the walls. The light danced across the high-polished mahogany paneling, concealing one of the world's most advanced security systems—a flawless marriage of centuries-old craftsmanship and cutting-edge technology.

The air was thick with history and power, tinged with the faint scent of beeswax from handmade candles and the distinct aroma of aged mahogany. Around the massive conference table of black Sicilian marble—its surface so polished it reflected the chandelier's light like a midnight lake—sat the twelve members of the Shadow Council in heavy silence.

Malaconda stood motionless by the room's only "window," a technological marvel projecting a seamless real-time view of Paris from the perspective of the Eiffel Tower. His silver-gray hair gleamed in the artificial light, and his tailored Brioni suit clung perfectly to his lean frame. In his hand, he held an untouched glass of 1926 Macallan, the deep amber liquid catching and refracting the chandelier's light.

"The situation in Berlin has... evolved beyond our original parameters," his voice was soft as velvet, yet carried an undertone of surgical steel that made several Council members instinctively straighten in their seats. The faint echo of his words bounced between the walls of the subterranean chamber.

"Shinkelhof is displaying increasing signs of mental instability. Novus, as expected, has breached the security systems. And Prometheus..." He turned slowly toward the table, his movements deliberate and precise, "is exhibiting behavioral patterns none of our models predicted."

"We must terminate the entire operation immediately," Miyazaki, the Japanese representative and CEO of Asia's largest technology conglomerate, leaned forward. His usually stoic face was marked with worry, beads of sweat glistening on his forehead under the dim light. "Risk assessments indicate—"

"Risk assessments?" Volkov's low laugh echoed eerily through the chamber, amplified by the acoustics into something almost inhuman. The hulking Russian delegate's massive frame made the antique chair beneath him groan in protest. "We stand on the brink of total control over global information management. This is hardly the time for academic concerns, dear Miyazaki. Think of the power Prometheus could grant us. Think of the technological leap—and the profit."

"If Novus succeeds in exposing our involvement..." Dr. Klaus, former head of the German intelligence agency, let the sentence hang in the air like an invisible threat. His fingers drummed nervously on the marble table's dark surface. "Our political contacts cannot protect us if the truth comes out."

Malaconda raised a hand in a nearly imperceptible gesture. Silence fell instantly—decades of conditioning had taught the Council members to heed even his slightest signals.

"My dear friends and colleagues," his voice now carried an almost hypnotic quality, "it is for moments like these that the Shadow Council exists. We are men and women who dare risk everything for success. Shinkelhof has taken... liberties, yes, but he has done so to ensure his company's survival." His thin smile sent a shiver down the spine of the Brazilian delegate.

"And Dr. Rossi?" Madame DuBois' voice cut through the air as she examined her perfectly manicured nails in the chandelier's light. "The Genesis implant? Her... unexpected connection to the project?"

"An unforeseen complication, I admit." Malaconda gently placed his untouched whiskey on the table and activated a holographic display. Streams of complex data and neural patterns danced like ghostly blue fireflies over the black marble surface. "But perhaps also our greatest opportunity. Observe these patterns..."

As he outlined his plan, some Council members visibly paled with horror, while others smiled with chilling approval. Dr. Klaus discreetly dabbed sweat from his brow with a silk handkerchief. Miyazaki's knuckles whitened as he clenched his hands beneath the table. Volkov nodded appreciatively, his eyes glittering with a hunger that was unmistakable.

"This is madness," whispered the Indian delegate, her voice trembling. "Absolute madness."

"No, my friend," Malaconda's smile grew as he projected the next phase of the plan. The holograms cast an eerie blue glow over his aristocratic features. "This is the future. *Our* future."

Outside the technological window, Paris glittered in the night, millions of tiny lights mirroring the stars above. The city's residents remained blissfully unaware that their fate—and the fate of the world—was being debated in a medieval chamber deep beneath their feet, where history's most powerful shadow organization prepared to transition from influence to absolute control.

"One last thing," Malaconda's voice cut through the silence like a finely honed blade. "If anyone wishes to withdraw from the project... now is the time to speak." His icy gaze swept methodically across the table. "I assure you, you will leave the Council with... your dignity intact."

No one moved. No one even dared to breathe.

"Excellent." With an elegant wave of his hand, he activated the next hologram. "Let us proceed to the operation's final phase."

54

Hotel Adlon, Berlin, Germany

Red warning lights pulsed hypnotically on the holographic display in front of an increasingly desperate Shinkelhof. The elegant interior of the presidential suite—with its crystal chandeliers and handwoven Persian rugs worth millions—had been transformed into an improvised high-tech laboratory. The acrid scent of electronics and ozone mingled with the faint perfume of the room's luxurious furnishings. A half-dozen of the world's foremost scientists, clad in white lab coats, moved between workstations with a quiet efficiency born of years of expertise—and a deep, gnawing sense of unease.

"The biological metrics are continuing to decline," Dr. Zhang reported, her fingers flying over the holographic controls. Beads of sweat glistened on her forehead in the pulsing red light of the warning displays. "The battery level is critically low, sir. We must find a stable power source immediately, or we risk permanent tissue damage."

"This is completely impossible," hissed Shinkelhof as his trembling hands attempted to calibrate the stabilizers. His once immaculate appearance was in tatters—the expensive shirt soaked with sweat, the hand-stitched silk tie hanging loosely around his neck, his bloodshot eyes a testament to sleepless nights and mounting panic. The room reeked of fear and cold sweat.

"Dr. Weber," he barked over the cacophony of humming electronics and warning tones, "we need to recalibrate the biomechanical connections immediately. Increase the power supply by twenty percent."

"But sir," Weber protested, his round glasses reflecting the pulsing red of the warning lights, "at that level, we'll risk irreversible damage to the biological components. The tissue is already under extreme stress from the unstable power supply."

At the panoramic window, Gavrail stood motionless, his muscular frame taut beneath his tailored suit. His icy gaze shifted methodically between the scientists' frantic work and the city traffic below, forty floors down. Berlin was coming to life in the dawn's light, blissfully unaware of the drama unfolding in the skyscraper's uppermost reaches.

Suddenly, Dr. Zhang's eyes lit up. "Wait... I see a pattern here." She projected a complex holographic model of the prototype's internal systems into the air. "If we synchronize the power input with the biological components' natural rhythm…"

"Yes!" Weber leaned forward eagerly. "Like a pacemaker—we match the energy pulses to the system's own frequency!"

Shinkelhof rushed to the control panel, his eyes wide with a glimmer of hope. "Do it. Now!"

Dr. Zhang began inputting commands with lightning precision. The red warning lights gradually shifted to yellow, then green. A low, harmonious hum replaced the shrill alarms.

"Battery levels are rising," reported Dr. Müller, his voice tinged with growing excitement. "Twenty percent… thirty… thirty-five…"

"Biological metrics are stabilizing," Weber confirmed, his eyes glued to the diagnostics. "The tissue is starting to regenerate. It… it's actually working!"

"Forty-five percent!" Zhang exclaimed triumphantly. "We have stable power!"

Shinkelhof collapsed into a leather armchair, this time out of sheer relief. His hands still trembled, but now with exhilaration rather than despair. "We did it," he whispered. "We actually have a chance to…"

"Time until the press conference?" Gavrail's cold voice cut through the room from his position at the window.

"One hour and forty-five minutes," Zhang replied as she monitored the now-stable systems. "At this charge level… we can do it. We can actually present Prometheus to the world."

Outside the windows, the sun rose over Berlin, its first rays striking the distant Brandenburg Gate. This time, it wasn't just the looming threat of a deadline—it was the promise of a new dawn, a new era on the horizon.

In the presidential suite, the scientists methodically prepared for the presentation, their expressions now marked by cautious optimism rather than desperation.

Shinkelhof adjusted his tie and took a deep breath. "Let's show the world what Prometheus is truly capable of."

55

Hotel Adlon, Berlin, Germany

In the gray dawn behind Hotel Adlon's grand façade, Hugo and Sussie maneuvered through the discreet service entrance, their cover identities as Deutsche Telekom technicians flawless down to the smallest detail. The navy uniforms with the company logo were identical to the genuine staff's, complete with the correct ID badges clipped to their chest pockets. The bustling activity of kitchen staff preparing breakfast provided natural cover as they navigated the fluorescent-lit service corridors.

"Thermal scans show six armed guards on this level," Sussie whispered, studying her camouflaged tablet that appeared to be an ordinary work computer. The blue coveralls skillfully concealed her tactical gear and the compact MP7 slung at her side. "Gavrail's men are moving in a routine pattern—thirty-second intervals between each checkpoint. Almost military precision."

"Fredrika, status update," Hugo activated his comms as they waited for a group of bleary-eyed cleaners to pass with their carts. His hand rested lightly on the concealed SIG Sauer beneath his uniform.

"Madeleine has just activated Protocol Midnight from Malmö," Fredrika's voice came through the encrypted channel. "Phase one initiates in exactly twenty minutes. Team Two, under Sarah Chen, has secured their position at the east entrance disguised as a *Financial Times* delegation. Team Three has gained access to the roof via the ventilation system."

They reached a hidden service elevator absent from the hotel's official blueprints—an artifact of the building's complex history. Sussie discreetly connected a quantum hacking device to the control panel while Hugo scanned the corridor with trained vigilance.

The elevator carried them methodically up to the technical service level just above the conference floor. Through dusty ventilation grates, they could see an increasing number of journalists gathering in the opulent hall below. With surgical precision, Sussie placed the first microphone, perfectly camouflaged as a standard maintenance device.

"Gavrail has doubled security around the presidential suite," she noted. "Count on a minimum of four heavily armed guards."

Hugo checked his silenced SIG Sauer one last time, feeling its reassuring weight. "Exact timing for Madeleine's signal?"

"Fifteen minutes until Protocol Midnight activates. Be ready— when the system goes live, everything will escalate quickly. We'll have one chance, no more."

They continued their systematic infiltration as the morning sun slowly climbed over Berlin's rooftops, gilding the columns of the Brandenburg Gate in the distance. Beneath them, they could feel the tension in the conference hall mounting with every passing minute. None of the gathered journalists, busy setting up their cameras and preparing their notes, suspected that they were about to witness something entirely different from the technological revolution they anticipated.

"Critical update," Fredrika's voice suddenly cut through the radio silence. "Our contact at Tegel Airport confirms Malaconda has just landed in his private Gulfstream. Estimated arrival at the hotel: thirty minutes."

Hugo and Sussie exchanged a long look, a silent exchange that spoke of years of shared experience. The game had just become exponentially more complicated.

"Adjust operational parameters," Hugo commanded, activating his team through the secure channel.

He didn't need to finish the sentence. They all knew that the fate of the world could be decided within this building over the coming hours.

Above them, the hotel's clock struck eight, its deep chime a solemn reminder that time was slipping away.

56

Hotel Adlon, Berlin, Germany

The grand conference hall of Hotel Adlon buzzed with tense anticipation. Over a hundred journalists and financial analysts crowded before the elevated podium as the morning sun poured through the tall leaded windows, casting rainbow-like reflections from the crystal chandeliers onto the elegant space. Cameras flashed in a constant storm of light, and the assembled microphones from the world's leading news agencies pointed at the empty lectern like an arsenal of black spears.

Behind the burgundy stage curtains, Shinkelhof was drenched in sweat as his assistant, Weber, frantically attempted to straighten his Italian silk tie. His hands trembled so violently that he could barely hold the titanium-encased presentation tablet. Beside him stood the Prometheus prototype, securely encased in its custom-designed housing, while two technicians made final adjustments with focused precision.

"Two minutes to curtain call," Gavrail's low voice came through his concealed earpiece. His elite security team had already taken up carefully selected positions around the hall, concealed weapons ready beneath their impeccably tailored suits. "Is the system stabilized for the demonstration?"

"It... it has to be stable enough," Shinkelhof stammered, his eyes fixed on the alarming energy graphs on his tablet screen. "There's no turning back now. Malaconda is already..."

The words caught in his throat as his mind raced through the implications of failure.

*

High above the venue in the technical service area, Hugo and Sussie observed the scene below through dusty ventilation grates. The heat from the spotlight system caused sweat to drip down their backs as they maintained their positions.

"Team Two, status update," Hugo whispered into his comm, his eyes scanning the positions of the security personnel.

"Position secured," Sarah Chen responded from her vantage point among the journalists. "I have visual on the target. West exit is under control."

"Team Three, report?"

"Roof neutralized," came the muted reply.

On stage, a ripple of spontaneous applause broke out as the host, a well-known German tech journalist, stepped forward to introduce the day's keynote speaker. Shinkelhof adjusted his Brioni jacket one last time, clutching the prototype's case tightly, his pupils dilated from the stimulants coursing through his system.

"Ladies and gentlemen," the host's voice echoed through the sophisticated sound system, "it is with great joy and pride that I present Dr. Reinhart Shinkelhof, founder and CEO of Shinkelhof Medical, here to unveil something that will change how we see the world... quite literally."

As Shinkelhof stepped into the blinding spotlight, his face a mask of forced confidence, Madeleine activated the clandestine Protocol Midnight from her secure position in Malmö.

A cascade of hidden commands began to infiltrate the hotel's network, spreading silently and systematically.

No one in the packed conference hall suspected that the countdown to chaos had just begun.

57

Hotel Adlon, Berlin, Germany

"...and now, ladies and gentlemen," Shinkelhof gestured with trembling hands toward the floating holographic display behind him, where intricate neural patterns danced in mid-air, "I will demonstrate how *Prometheus* is set to revolutionize the entire interface between humans and machines. A technology that will forever change how we interact with information."
His unsteady hands carefully lifted the prototype from its cryogenic container. The gathered journalists leaned forward in their chairs, pens and microphones poised to document what could become a historic moment. The air buzzed with anticipation, the clicks of hundreds of cameras echoing through the elegant hall.
"What began as a visionary research project within Shinkelhof Medical—internally referred to as *Codename Vision*—has now evolved into something far beyond our original hopes," he continued, his voice growing stronger, more assured. "Imagine a world where the boundary between thought and action dissolves. Where our intentions are directly translated into digital reality. That is precisely what *Prometheus* offers." He raised the container into the light, revealing the pulsing blue energy swirling within. "This is not just another AI, nor merely another neural network. This is something entirely different."
He began to move across the stage, confidence returning to his stride. "*Prometheus* combines advanced quantum computing with biosynthetic neural linkages. It doesn't just learn—it grows, adapts, evolves. It doesn't merely understand commands—it comprehends intentions, emotions, context."
On the massive screen behind him, a cascade of holographic visuals exploded, demonstrating the system's complexity.
"Observe how the neural linkages form in real time, how the system responds to the slightest thought, the faintest impulse.

With *Prometheus*, we are no longer confined by keyboards, screens, or voice commands. We can interact with the digital world as naturally as moving our own limbs."

His eyes glowed with an almost feverish intensity. "When we launched the *Vision* project, we scarcely dared to dream of these possibilities—in medicine, where surgeons can perform operations at the speed of thought. In education, where teachers can share knowledge directly, mind-to-mind. In research, where scientists can visualize and manipulate complex data using sheer brainpower."

Shinkelhof paused dramatically as the holograms behind him pulsed in hypnotic patterns. "But this is only the beginning. *Prometheus* is not merely a tool—it is the next step in human evolution. A bridge between the organic and the digital. A gateway to a future where our mental capabilities expand beyond anything we've ever imagined."

He lifted the prototype higher, its blue glow reflecting in his wide pupils. "Today, we take the first step into this new era. Today, we show the world that what was once science fiction, a mere vision, is now reality. And now..." he smiled triumphantly as he prepared for the demonstration, "I will show you exactly what *Prometheus* can do."

The hall held its breath. Hundreds of eyes were fixed on the pulsing prototype in his hands. The majestic silhouette of the Brandenburg Gate loomed through the tall windows behind him, a silent witness to what might be the dawn of a new era in human history.

Gavrail, stationed discreetly at the eastern side entrance in his tailored suit, suddenly noticed a movement that broke the expected pattern. *Financial Times* reporter Sarah Chen in the third row—her right hand moved toward her laptop bag with a precision only years of specialized training could produce.

"Sector three, potential threat identified," he hissed into his microphone. "Initiate protocol—"

The muffled crack of a Sig Sauer fitted with a professional suppressor sliced through the air like a sharp knife. The bullet struck the podium mere centimeters from Shinkelhof's trembling hand, shattering the polished wood in an explosive spray of splinters. *Prometheus* slipped from his faltering grasp, the device clattering to the stage floor with a metallic ring. Panic erupted instantly in the crowded hall. The crystal chandeliers sparkled under the harsh stage lights as journalists scrambled for the exits. Gavrail's trained security team drew their concealed weapons with flawless coordination. Shinkelhof stood paralyzed on stage, his wide eyes fixed on the smoking splinter where the projectile had struck, so close to his fingers he could feel its residual heat.

"Secure the prototype immediately!" Gavrail's commanding voice cut through the chaos as he dashed toward the podium, gun drawn. But then another shot rang out from an entirely different angle—a textbook crossfire tactic that sent the security personnel diving for cover.

From his strategic position in the ventilation shaft, Hugo watched as Sarah Chen moved toward the stage with the precision of an elite operator, her fake press credentials discarded as the cover they had been. Meanwhile, Sussie beside him activated the first phase of Protocol Midnight—and suddenly, every light in the grand hall extinguished, emergency lighting included.

In the compact darkness, the air filled with panicked screams intermingled with methodical gunfire. The sounds echoed eerily off the walls as people stumbled over each other in desperation. Somewhere in the tumult, Shinkelhof's hysterical voice rose above the clamor:

"You don't understand! If the power fails... if the cooling systems shut down... the entire system will... no, NO!"

Gavrail's sharp orders to his team were drowned out by the sound of shattering glass as the first windows succumbed to the pressure of the panicked crowd. Morning light streamed through the broken panes, casting surreal shadows over the chaos in the hall.

"Hugo," Sussie's voice was tense in his earpiece. "Energy readings are at critical levels. Something's happening to the power supply—"

A deafening sound, somewhere between an explosion and an electrical discharge, shook the entire hall. The air filled with ozone and the acrid smell of burning electronics. The darkness seemed to deepen as the backup generators overloaded and failed with a series of sharp pops.
And then the real battle began.

58

Hotel Adlon, Berlin, Germany

The dim glow of the emergency lighting cast surreal shadows across the chaotic conference hall, transforming the elegant walls into a landscape of shifting forms. The prisms of the chandeliers fractured the sparse light into ghostly patterns over the panicked journalists huddled beneath the polished conference tables. Gavrail directed his team with precise hand signals as they methodically attempted to establish a secure evacuation corridor toward the eastern emergency exit. Shinkelhof stood trembling on the bullet-riddled podium, his once-pristine suit now soaked with sweat and dust from the splintered wood. His bloodshot eyes darted frantically between the exits, his hands twisting compulsively as though trying to wring clarity from the chaos.

"The west exit is completely compromised," Nico reported through the encrypted comms, his usually calm voice tinged with stress. "We've got no—"

A fresh, well-coordinated volley of silenced gunfire cut him off. Bullets with specialized dampened tips thudded into the walls, leaving perfect holes in the hand-painted wallpaper. The air grew thick with the acrid smell of gunpowder and plaster dust. Shinkelhof's panicked gaze swept the room until it landed on a young BBC journalist, Catherine Walsh, who was still attempting to document the chaos with her camera. With surprising speed for a man in his condition, he lunged forward and seized the woman. "Back off! I see you! One step closer, and she dies right here and now!"

"An exceptionally poor choice, Doctor," Gavrail's voice sliced through the room, cold and precise as a scalpel. He struggled to push through the crush of fleeing journalists toward Hugo and Sussie, who moved like shadows through the turmoil. "Release the woman. Immediately."

Shinkelhof's remaining security team worked frantically to barricade the double doors with heavy conference furniture, while terrified journalists crouched beneath tables, abandoning cameras and microphones on the floor.

"It's over, Shinkelhof. Let her go," Hugo's authoritative voice echoed through the hall. He and Sussie advanced methodically, every step underpinned by years of training. "You must understand there's no way out of this. Not anymore."

"You don't understand anything!" Shinkelhof pressed the Glock harder against the hostage's temple, his hand shaking so violently that the safety scraped against her skin. Sweat poured down his face in rivulets, and his eyes gleamed with a feverish intensity, betraying a man teetering on the brink of collapse. "Back off! I said, back off!"

Gavrail struggled to navigate through the throng, his frustration clear in the steely determination of his gray eyes as he saw Hugo and Sussie closing in on Shinkelhof. "Stop!" he shouted, but his command was swallowed by the chaos of fleeing people and overturned furniture.

Another burst of gunfire echoed through the room, and more glass shattered somewhere in the darkness. Screams of panic merged with the cacophony of running footsteps. Amid the turmoil, Shinkelhof stood his ground with his hostage, his face twisted in a grotesque mask of desperation and madness.

The tension in the room was now so thick it felt tangible. Hugo and Sussie pressed forward relentlessly, their movements calculated and unwavering. Meanwhile, Gavrail fought to reach them in time, ensnared in a tide of panicked humanity.

All the while, the surreal interplay of flickering emergency lights and shifting shadows seemed to cast the unfolding standoff into the realm of a nightmare—one from which no one could awaken.

59

Hotel Adlon, Berlin, Germany

Dr. Elena Rossi rose to her full height, her posture radiating an authority that made even Gavrail's elite operatives flinch. The prisms of the chandeliers refracted the dim emergency lighting into a pattern of shifting shadows across the walls.

"You always misunderstood one fundamental thing, Reinhart," Dr. Rossi's voice carried a precision that cut through the chaos, clinical and sharp as a surgical laser. "*Prometheus* was never your creation. It was always mine—the result of decades of research that you so elegantly appropriated."

"Elena..." Shinkelhof spun around so quickly he nearly lost his balance, his face pale with shock. Beads of sweat glistened on his forehead under the emergency lights. "How... how dare you come here?"

"How dare *you* steal my life's work?" She stepped forward, her eyes cold as steel. "Did you truly think I would sit quietly while you presented my innovation as your own? While you twisted decades of my research into a mere product demonstration?"

"You don't understand," Shinkelhof protested, his voice trembling with desperation. "Your theories... your experiments... they needed resources, funding, a vision—"

"My vision," Rossi interrupted with icy precision. "Not yours. I spent twenty years developing the neural linkages. Fifteen years perfecting the biosynthetic interfaces. A lifetime of dedicated research that you tried to steal in a single night."

Around them, the journalists stood frozen, their cameras and microphones trained on the unexpected drama unfolding before them. Hugo and Sussie moved discreetly through the shadows, ready to act at the first sign of violence.

"You could never have brought it to fruition!" Shinkelhof gestured wildly toward the prototype. "You were trapped in your lab, lost in theories and equations. I gave *Prometheus* life! I made it real!"

"Real? You're delusional." Rossi's laugh was bitter. "You took my prototypes, even the codename *Vision*—everything I built over decades—and thought you could grasp its true essence? You're no visionary, Reinhart. You're a thief who stumbled onto something you couldn't understand."

Gavrail struggled to push through the crowd, but the journalists, eager to capture every moment of the confrontation, made it impossible to reach the stage.

"You're ruining everything!" Shinkelhof's voice cracked with desperation. "This is bigger than you and me! Think of the possibilities, the progress—"

"Progress built on stolen dreams is no progress at all," Rossi countered. "You never understood the fundamental principle behind *Prometheus*. It's not about control or profit—it's about understanding the true nature of human consciousness."

Her words echoed through the silent hall as hundreds of cameras recorded every moment. Shinkelhof stood there, his once-imposing figure now slumped and defeated, as the truth of his theft was laid bare for the world to see.

"It's over, Reinhart," Dr. Rossi said finally, her voice softer now but still resolute. "Let the world know the truth. It's the least you owe to everyone involved."

In the tense silence that followed, the weight of her words sank in among the assembled journalists. The sound of their feverish reporting swelled, a crescendo of revelation that filled the room. Gavrail raised his weapon.

60

Hotel Adlon, Berlin, Germany

The rhythmic thrum of rotor blades sent the antique crystal chandeliers into sympathetic vibrations as the matte-black Bell 412 helicopter, custom-modified for the Shadow Council's covert operations, touched down on the historic roof of Hotel Adlon. Wind whipped dust and gravel into miniature cyclones around the landing zone. Malaconda stepped into the cold Berlin air with his signature elegance, his Savile Row suit immaculate despite the turbulence. Behind him emerged six operatives from the Shadow Council's elite strike team, their black tactical gear seeming to absorb all light.

"Secure the perimeter," he commanded, adjusting his platinum cufflinks with meticulous care. "I want full control over all exits within two minutes. Initiate Omega Protocol immediately," he ordered into his comms, backing toward the nearest exit.

"Activate all charges. No delay."

"Sir, a full detonation will destabilize the entire structure. The collapse will be total."

"Precisely the point."

Throughout the historic building, carefully placed explosive charges began their countdown sequences. Red LED lights blinked rhythmically in ventilation shafts, behind antique panels, beneath marble floors—a hidden constellation of destruction waiting for its signal.

The operatives moved with silent precision, their every step a testament to elite training. On the roof, Malaconda lit a cigarette, the faint glow illuminating his face for a brief moment as he took a measured drag. The chaos inside the building would soon cascade into the perfect storm of destruction he had meticulously orchestrated.

"Remember," he added coldly into his comms, "no witnesses."

61

Hotel Adlon, Berlin, Germany

The legendary lobby of Hotel Adlon, once a monument to European luxury and refinement, transformed in seconds into an apocalyptic battleground. Bullets tore through the hand-painted French wallpaper in violent explosions of plaster and pigment, while panicked journalists desperately sought shelter behind the massive pillars of Italian Carrara marble. The gigantic crystal chandelier, an original design from 1907, shattered under the force of a well-aimed shot from Gavrail's Sig Sauer, raining down onto the polished marble floor in a cascade of prismatic glitter and lethal shards.

Thick black smoke began pouring from the ventilation system, and the fire alarm blared with an ear-splitting wail that echoed throughout the chaotic lobby.

"Hold the left flank!" Hugo shouted as he methodically pushed Gavrail and his bodyguards back toward the gilded double doors of the restaurant. His precisely aimed shots forced the opposition to duck behind the reception desk. "They're trying to reach the service corridor! Sussie, update on evacuation status!"

On the balcony above the lobby, Malaconda watched the scene with mounting fury. His normally composed face twisted into a mask of cold rage as he saw Shinkelhof failing to control the situation. All the planning, the millions in investment—everything was unraveling before his eyes.

"You incompetent fool," he hissed, gripping the balustrade so tightly his knuckles whitened. "You had one job, Shinkelhof."

"Sir," one of his black-clad operatives leaned forward, voice tense. "Shall we initiate the evacuation protocol?"

Malaconda turned slowly to the operative, his eyes cold as winter steel. "No. Instead, initiate Protocol Omega Black. Burn the entire building to the ground. Shinkelhof has outlived his usefulness—ensure he doesn't leave the building alive."

"But sir, the press, the civilians—"

"Are acceptable losses." Malaconda's voice was icy and deliberate. "No one must know the truth of what happened here today. Activate the charges on all floors. Let the fire erase our tracks."

Below, the chaos continued to escalate. Shinkelhof, clutching the *Prometheus* prototype to his chest with an almost reverent grip, let out a manic laugh that echoed eerily between the columns. Smoke from the overheating power systems grew thicker, and sparks flew from the short-circuiting panels.

"You still don't understand!" he screamed, sweat streaming down his soot-streaked face. "This is evolution! The next step in technology!"

"Idiot," Malaconda muttered, activating his secure comms. "Team Alpha, eliminate the target. Immediately."

Snipers began taking precise positions around the lobby as the smoke thickened. The fire alarm blared incessantly, and sprinklers had activated on several floors, creating a surreal rain over the ongoing battle.

"Sir," a technician reported, "the charges are armed. Timed for detonation in six minutes."

"Perfect." Malaconda adjusted his platinum cufflinks with surgical precision. "Let it burn. Let it all burn. And make sure Shinkelhof burns with it."

Below him, the battle intensified as the smoke thickened. The fire alarm's wail continued unabated, and through the growing haze, he could see his elite team methodically positioning themselves for the final assault.

"The fire is spreading!" Sussie shouted over the comms. "We have multiple hotspots across three floors. The building needs to be evacuated immediately!"

Malaconda allowed himself a thin, cold smile as he backed toward his private exit. Behind him, the first sniper shots echoed through the lobby, followed by panicked screams and the sound of more shattered glass.

"Sometimes," he murmured to himself, brushing an invisible speck of dust from his sleeve, "you must sacrifice a pawn to win the game. Farewell, Shinkelhof. You were always... replaceable." Somewhere in the heart of the building, the hidden charges ticked inexorably toward zero, while the rising smoke curled toward the ceiling, transforming the once-majestic lobby into an infernal warzone.

"The helicopter is ready, sir," his bodyguard reported.

"Excellent. Let us witness the end of this... failed demonstration from a safe distance."

62

Hotel Adlon, Berlin, Germany

The award-winning Lorenz Restaurant at Hotel Adlon, once a haven of refined fine dining with its two Michelin stars, had in mere seconds transformed into a surreal warzone. The handwoven white damask tablecloths turned crimson from spilled Château Lafite and darker stains of blood, while exclusive Riedel crystal shattered under the panicked stiletto heels of Louboutin-clad patrons. The air hung heavy with the acrid tang of cordite, mingled with thick black smoke and the abandoned scents of Wagyu beef and lobster thermidor from abruptly interrupted business lunches.

"Against the wall! Everyone to the outer wall, now!" shouted headwaiter Franz as he desperately tried to direct terrified guests away from the intensifying crossfire. His once impeccably starched tuxedo was now spattered with wine and flecks of shattered glass. A stray 9mm round struck the antique champagne shelf behind the carved mahogany bar, sending an array of Dom Pérignon Vintage 2008 bottles exploding in a decadent cascade of froth and Venetian crystal shards.

The fire alarm shrieked deafeningly, and thick smoke billowed from the ventilation system. Explosive sounds came from the kitchen, where overheated electronics short-circuited, and gas canisters began to expand ominously in the heat.

Gavrail's elite operatives had overturned the massive oak chairs into makeshift barricades with military precision, their tailored Brioni suits now dusted with shards of glass and splashes of '82 Bordeaux. They moved with disciplined choreography between the toppled French walnut tables, covering one another with the sharp professionalism that stood in stark contrast to the chaos surrounding them.

"It's over, Shinkelhof. Let go of Ms. Walsh," Hugo's voice cut through the cacophony of shattering porcelain and panicked screams. "You have literally nowhere to run. The building is surrounded, and the fire is spreading rapidly."

Shinkelhof, clutching BBC journalist Catherine Walsh in front of him as a human shield, edged step by step toward the swinging stainless-steel kitchen doors. His other hand gripped the Prometheus prototype with a near-reverent intensity, his wide, panicked eyes darting in every direction.

"You're all blind!" he yelled, his voice cracking as sweat dripped from his soot-streaked face and stained his once-pristine Thomas Pink shirt.

A new coordinated salvo from Gavrail's expertly trained team rattled the antique Baccarat chandeliers, their ominous clinking echoing throughout the room. An elderly German industrial magnate in a bespoke Savile Row suit and his wife in a Chanel ensemble huddled beneath a pierced Gustav III table, her triple-strand Cartier pearl necklace glinting in the flickering glow of the advancing flames.

"The fire is spreading rapidly through the ventilation system. The entire eastern wing is already engulfed," a voice reported over the comms.

Catherine Walsh, her journalistic instincts overriding even survival instinct, continued her report into a concealed microphone despite Shinkelhof's Glock pressed firmly to her temple. "We're in the midst of what is undoubtedly the most dramatic technological incident of the century. The smoke is growing thicker, and the temperature is rising fast. It sounds like the entire building is about to—"

A fresh explosion from the kitchen cut her off, sending a wave of searing heat crashing through the restaurant. The sprinklers hissed to life, creating a surreal rain that mingled with the chaos.

"Time for Plan B," Hugo muttered, signaling Sussie with the agreed-upon hand gesture. "Initiate on my mark."

No one, not even Gavrail's elite operatives, noticed the discreet waitress behind the bar who slowly raised a suppressed MP7 while methodically polishing an already spotless champagne glass. Her eyes, cold as winter steel, locked onto a precise point

43 centimeters to the left of Shinkelhof's trembling hand clutching Prometheus.

In the kitchen, industrial fans began shutting down one by one, allowing the smoke to spill ever thicker into the room. Through the rising haze, flames could be seen licking the ornate cornices, while the luxurious wallpaper blistered and buckled in the mounting heat.

"We've got maybe two minutes before this entire floor goes up," Sussie reported calmly. "And Malaconda is probably still here."

63

Hotel Adlon, Berlin, Germany

The industrial kitchen, typically a seamless symphony of Michelin-starred precision, had devolved into a smoke-filled labyrinth of mortal peril. Steam hissed angrily from overheated Gaggenau pressure cookers and abandoned sauce demi-glace reductions, while black smoke poured relentlessly from the ventilation shafts. Stainless steel Miele surfaces gleamed ghostlike in the flickering light of growing flames. The air was an oppressive mixture of saffron and garlic from forgotten bouillabaisse, burnt butter from empty skillets, the metallic tang of fresh blood, and the acrid stench of burning plastic and electronics.

Hugo rolled with trained precision as Gavrail's first strike slammed into the industrial workbench where his head had been a fraction of a second earlier. The thick stainless steel buckled under the impact like a tin can. Kitchen staff in once-pristine white Adlon jackets fled in terror, darting between tall counters, their frantic movements casting distorted shadows in the thickening smoke.

"Impressive reflexes," Gavrail noted, advancing methodically through the haze with the precision of a neurosurgeon. His Brioni suit, now stained with soot and blood, clung to his frame like a second skin. "But you cannot stop what's coming. This is the end for all of you."

A stray 9mm round struck a main gas line with a metallic clang, unleashing a torrent of yellow flames that roared upward, creating an inferno between them. The kitchen, with its gleaming German engineering, now resembled something from Dante's *Inferno*. In the flickering chaos, rows of German chef knives glinted on their magnetic strips, poised like surgical tools awaiting their turn.

"It's over, Gavrail," Hugo countered, deftly deflecting a lethal strike with a lifted silver serving tray. "The entire building is on fire. Even Malaconda must realize—"

"On the contrary, my dear Xavier." Gavrail's thin smile didn't reach his eyes. "Every second follows the protocol precisely. Even your presence here. Malaconda has already sentenced you all to death."

Their deadly dance continued, weaving through industrial stoves and Gastronorm stations. A young sous-chef hiding beneath a Rational oven crossed himself silently as they passed in their violent choreography. Somewhere in the haze, Shinkelhof screamed incoherently about technological perfection, sparks flying from the overheating *Prometheus* prototype clutched in his trembling hands.

"Fire spread is critical," Fredrika reported tensely in Hugo's earpiece. "The eastern stairwell has collapsed. We have a maximum of two minutes before the entire floor is engulfed."

Gavrail suddenly snatched a Damascus steel knife from the wall with the speed of a striking snake. Its hand-forged edge gleamed menacingly in the erratic light of the flames.

"Shall we settle this the old way?" he said, weighing the perfectly balanced blade in his hand with a killer's poise. "Like that night in Macau? Before... the incident?"

Hugo locked eyes with him through the drifting smoke, reading the controlled madness in Gavrail's gaze. "This time the ending will be different, Gavrail. This time there are no secrets left."

An overheated Palux pressure cooker exploded in the darkness with a deafening boom, spraying scalding bouillabaisse across the walls like arterial blood. At the same time, a series of muffled detonations echoed as Malaconda's charges began to detonate on the floors above them.

"Sir," Nico's tense voice crackled through the comms. "The roof is starting to give! The entire structure—"

His voice was drowned out by the roar of another explosion, this one closer. The building itself groaned under the strain, concrete and steel warping under the relentless heat.

"Beautiful, isn't it?" Gavrail took a step closer, the knife glinting in his hand as smoke and flames swirled around them. "How everything falls into place, exactly as Malaconda predicted. Even your attempt to stop it becomes part of... the annihilation." Through the smoke, they could hear the building collapsing around them, floor by floor, as the rhythmic roar of the fire grew into a deafening crescendo of destruction.

64

Hotel Adlon, Berlin, Germany

The service elevator's worn steel cabin groaned as it ascended through the hotel's hidden arteries, its antique mechanisms protesting against the sudden acceleration. Shinkelhof was pressed against the back wall, his once-pristine Thomas Pink shirt now stained with cold sweat and darker patches of blood. Thin spirals of smoke rose from the Prometheus prototype in his trembling hands, its overheating circuits sparking ominously. "Faster," he whispered maniacally to the machinery, his eyes wide with a blend of terror and madness. "Faster! Can't you feel it? The heat... the fire is spreading!"

He was right—thick black smoke was billowing up the elevator shaft, and the temperature was rising rapidly as flames devoured the building's ventilation system. The metal walls of the cabin had begun to radiate heat, scorching to the touch.

Ten floors above, Malaconda's black-clad special forces team moved like shadows through the opulent corridors, methodically securing the top floor. Their movements were perfectly coordinated through a silent system of hand signals, years of shared training evident in every precise step.

"Omega position established and secured," the team leader reported into his microphone. "All exits under control. Awaiting delivery of the package. Fire spread is following projected patterns."

In a half-abandoned service corridor three floors below, Dr. Elena Rossi struggled against the suffocating smoke. The blaring fire alarms were deafening, and through the corridor's windows, she could see flames licking up the façade several stories below. "Fredrika," she rasped into her encrypted comms, each word a struggle against the thickening smoke. "You have to stop them before the entire building collapses. The structure... it was never designed to withstand this level of heat. It's going to—"

A series of explosions from Malaconda's strategically placed charges rocked the building, throwing her against the wood-paneled wall. Through the growing haze, she saw cracks spiderwebbing across the ceiling above her.

"They're using the elevator shaft as a chimney," she managed between coughing fits. "When the fire reaches the top floor... the entire structure will—"

"Sixty seconds until the roof collapses," Fredrika's voice came through the comms, tight with controlled urgency. "Hugo and Sussie are moving to intercept, but time... time is running out."

A sudden shudder rippled through the entire building, causing the crystal chandeliers to jingle ominously before shattering in the heat. In the elevator, a manic grin spread across Shinkelhof's sweat-slicked face as he felt the rising temperature through his clothes.

"At last," he whispered to the prototype cradled in his arms. "At last, they'll understand. This isn't the end... it's the revolution. The next step in technology!"

"Sir," Malaconda's voice rang coldly through the elevator's intercom system. "Are you ready for the final demonstration?"

"More than ready," Shinkelhof's laugh bordered on hysteria. "There's no turning back now. Can't you feel it? Everything is changing!"

The elevator continued its relentless climb upward through the building's fiery nerve centers, as heat and smoke climbed to unbearable levels. On each floor, bewildered hotel guests watched smoke seeping through the cracks of the elevator doors, while firefighters desperately tried to evacuate the upper levels.

In the corridor, Dr. Rossi sank to her knees, overwhelmed by the suffocating smoke. "Please," she whispered to no one in particular, "stop them. Before it's too late. Before... before the whole building comes down."

Through the windows, she could see Berlin's fire brigade deploying their tallest ladders, but the flames had already climbed too high for them to reach. Above her, the ceiling groaned ominously, the sound of crumbling concrete and warping steel echoing down the corridor.

"Oh my God," she murmured as another explosion rocked the building.

65

Hotel Adlon, Berlin, Germany

The historic marble staircase of Hotel Adlon spiraled upward like a white serpent through the building's heart, each floor marked by hand-gilded Art Nouveau numerals, remnants of an era of imperial luxury. The hand-forged iron railings and gold-plated Art Deco details, lovingly restored after the war, now reflected the flickering glow of the flames rising from the floors below. Thick black smoke billowed upward, while echoes of precise gunfire ricocheted off the polished Italian Carrara marble walls—each shot a desecration of this timeless elegance.

"Contact, third pillar!" Gavrail's sharp command rang out from above.

Hugo and Sussie pressed themselves against the heated marble wall on the eighteenth floor, their breaths controlled and synchronized despite the exertion of the long climb and the suffocating smoke. Bullets from Gavrail's elite snipers, trained by Israeli special forces, rained down from carefully chosen positions two floors up. Marble fragments exploded around them in cascades of white dust, swirling like ghostly powder in the choking haze.

"Twenty seconds to the next tactical position," Sussie whispered as she methodically reloaded her MP7, her movements honed through thousands of repetitions. Beads of sweat ran down her soot-streaked face, carving trails through the grime. "If we coordinate the attack on their left flank, using the blind spot behind the Ionic column—"

"Negative," Hugo replied, his voice measured. "They've secured that sector with crossfire. But maybe—"

His analysis was interrupted by a violent explosion from below. The entire building trembled as another of Malaconda's charges detonated. Security doors flung wildly on their hinges in the hot air currents, surveillance cameras melted one by one, and the air conditioning system began circulating toxic smoke through its ducts.

"Dr. Rossi," Hugo activated his comms, which crackled ominously through the intensifying heat. "Status report. What's happening to the building?"

"The structure... it's starting to give way." Her voice was strained, almost feverish. "The fire is spreading faster than anticipated... we have maybe ten minutes before the entire upper section collapses..." Her words dissolved into a violent coughing fit, followed by static.

"Elena!" Hugo's voice sharpened with concern. "Stay stable. We need—"

"All units, immediate regroup!" Gavrail's commanding voice sliced through the chaos from above. "South staircase is fully engulfed! Cover the southwestern sector—they're trying to reach the service elevator!"

Another volley of gunfire, scattered in the dense smoke, sent marble dust raining down on them. Hugo seized the brief chaos to propel himself up the next flight of stairs in a series of perfectly calculated movements, his years of special operations training evident in every step. Sussie covered his advance with a controlled burst that forced the attackers to duck behind the massive pillars.

"They're desperately buying time," Hugo muttered as he secured his new position behind a twisted column. "While Shinkelhof takes the prototype toward—"

"The elevator! Look!" Sussie's sharp exclamation drew his gaze upward through the majestic center of the staircase. The antique service elevator was jerking upward like a wounded insect, its electronics faltering in the heat. Smoke leaked through the gilded seams of the doors.

A deafening crash made them instinctively duck—a crystal chandelier had finally succumbed to the intense heat, shattering in a cascade of glittering fragments.

"Time to end this," Hugo said, drawing his backup pistol—a dependable Sig Sauer P226 passed down from his father. "Dr. Rossi, how much time do we have before the roof collapses?"

"Ten minutes... maybe less," her voice broke between coughs. "The temperature... it's rising rapidly. The steel beams are starting to fail..."

"Hugo," Sussie's voice was tense. "The helicopter is approaching from the southeast. I can hear the rotor blades over the fire." Above them, the fire continued to spread as Berlin awoke to another autumn morning, unaware of the drama unfolding in the city's historic heart. The Brandenburg Gate loomed majestically through the tall windows, its quadriga gilded by the dawn light, reflecting the growing flames.

Somewhere above, Shinkelhof's manic laughter echoed off the walls, blending with the growing roar of helicopter rotors and the relentless drumbeat of the fire.

Time was literally running out as Hotel Adlon's historic structure inexorably succumbed to the raging inferno.

66

Hotel Adlon, Berlin, Germany

The massive double doors of the presidential suite, crafted from French walnut, burst open with an explosive crash as Shinkelhof stumbled inside. His once-immaculate Savile Row suit was now a tattered ruin of sweat, blood, and marble dust. Through the arched windows, flames licked at the façade several floors below, while thick black smoke poured in through the ventilation system.

Malaconda stood motionless by the grand panoramic window, a dark silhouette against Berlin's dawn. His tailored Brioni suit remained impeccably pressed, as though the chaos below belonged to a separate reality altogether.

"You look... somewhat indisposed, dear Reinhart," his voice was smooth as aged cognac but carried an undertone of arctic cold that seemed to lower the room's temperature. "And our little prototype doesn't appear to be faring much better. The power supply is practically fried."

Shinkelhof clutched the prototype in a desperate grip. Around them, the Shadow Council's black-clad operatives moved like choreographed phantoms, securing every conceivable exit with trained precision.

"It doesn't matter!" Shinkelhof's voice was hoarse with madness and exhaustion. "This is only the beginning! A new era of technology! Can't you see the potential?"

"What I see," Malaconda turned slowly from the window, his movements predatory and deliberate, "is a pathetic man who has failed. Again. Just like Zurich. Just like Project Oracle. Your incompetence has cost us billions, Reinhart. And worse—you've exposed the entire operation."

A violent explosion shook the top floor to its foundations as another of Malaconda's charges detonated. Crystal glass shattered, furniture overturned, and through the corridor, the sound of panicked hotel guests being evacuated by security personnel echoed.

"Sir," one of the operatives, his face hidden behind a tactical mask, snapped to position by the main entrance. "Xavier and his team are advancing via the eastern staircase. Estimated arrival: two minutes. Gavrail's men report heavy resistance."

"Initiate Perimeter Beta," Malaconda commanded in the same tone one might use to order a fine wine. "Prepare the roof for immediate extraction. And Reinhart..." his immaculately manicured hand slipped beneath his tailored jacket, "put the prototype down. Slowly and carefully. You're wasting my valuable time."

"You still don't understand!" Shinkelhof backed against the brocade-covered wall as the fire alarms shrieked and the sprinklers hissed to life. "I've created something revolutionary! Something that will change the world! You're too blind to—"

"Blind?" Malaconda's voice sliced through the air like a scalpel. His hand emerged, now holding a matte-black, customized Glock 18. "No, Reinhart. *You're* the blind one. So lost in your delusions of grandeur that you fail to see the obvious—you've outlived your usefulness. You're a defective component that must be... removed."

"You can't kill me," Shinkelhof hissed, his eyes wide with panic and insanity. "I'm the only one who understands the technology! The only one who—"

"You were never more than a tool," Malaconda interrupted icily. "A useful but replaceable tool. And like all tools, there comes a time when they must be... discarded. Your time is up, Reinhart."

Another explosion rocked the floor. Through the windows, they could see the fire reaching the upper levels, transforming the historic façade into an inferno of orange flames against the dawn sky.

"Beautiful," Shinkelhof whispered, tears cutting streaks through the soot on his cheeks. "Everything I built... everything I created..."

"And it will all burn," Malaconda concluded with a thin smile. "With you."

67

Hotel Adlon, Berlin, Germany

The exclusive rooftop terrace of Hotel Adlon, where Berlin's political and financial elite usually sipped vintage Dom Pérignon under pristine evening skies, had been transformed into an apocalyptic battlefield. Dawn's first light broke over the city's dramatic silhouette in the east as two matte-black Bell 412 helicopters circled above like predatory birds. Their powerful rotors churned the smoke-filled morning air into swirling mini-storms, toppling elegantly set breakfast tables and scattering napkins and crystal glasses in chaotic patterns across the terrace.

Police sirens echoed through the streets below, joined by the approaching wails of fire engines. Thick black smoke billowed from the lower floors, climbing relentlessly toward the rooftop. Behind massive ventilation units and neoclassical statues, Malaconda's elite snipers had taken up strategic positions. Their carbon-fiber tactical uniforms blended seamlessly with the shadows as the morning sun gilded the Brandenburg Gate in the distance. Through the thickening smoke, flames could be seen licking up the hotel's façade, devouring the historic structure floor by floor.

"Secure the perimeter at all costs!" Malaconda's commanding voice cut through the roaring wind and the rhythmic thrum of the rotor blades. "No one boards the extraction helicopter until the package is secured!"

A precisely coordinated volley from Hugo's position behind an antique chimney forced one of Malaconda's snipers to duck with millimeter precision. Meanwhile, Sussie had claimed a commanding spot behind a neoclassical copper water reservoir, her modified MP7 covering the entire eastern sector of the terrace with surgical accuracy.

"They're moving toward primary extraction point Alpha," she reported through the crackling comms. "Shinkelhof is heading for the north—"

Her report was interrupted by Dr. Rossi's dramatic emergence from the antique stairwell. Her lab coat was streaked with soot, and her face bore the marks of exhaustion and desperation.

"Reinhart, for God's sake, stop!" Dr. Rossi's voice carried over the rising winds and the wailing sirens. "The building is collapsing! We have minutes before the entire structure fails!"

A violent explosion from the floor below shook the rooftop terrace. In the heart of the chaos stood Shinkelhof, his once-dignified face twisted into an expression of near-religious madness as he clutched the smoking Prometheus prototype to his chest.

"You understand nothing!" he laughed, his voice trembling with hysteria. "This is only the beginning! A new era of technology! Let it burn! Let it all burn!"

"You're insane," Malaconda hissed, leveling his suppressed Glock with unerring precision. "The entire operation is compromised. All the planning—all the resources—wasted."

"Planning?" Shinkelhof's laughter echoed across the terrace. "We stand at the precipice of technological revolution, and you speak of planning?"

Malaconda's expertly trained operatives opened fire in a perfectly coordinated volley as the larger Bell 412 helicopter swung in for landing, its powerful searchlights cutting through the smoke pouring up from the blazing floors below.

"Oh my God," Sussie whispered, peering through her scope as she watched the eastern façade begin to crumble under the relentless heat. "The entire east wing is collapsing."

The police sirens grew louder, and through the smoke, firefighters' ladders rose toward the burning structure in a desperate attempt to reach the upper floors. Berlin collectively held its breath as its most iconic hotel transformed into a towering inferno.

"Stop him," Dr. Rossi's voice was barely more than a whisper. "Before he takes the entire building down with him. Before everything we've worked for is lost in the flames."

Another explosion rocked the structure to its core. Through the haze, they could see Malaconda's helicopter maneuvering for landing, its rotor blades whipping the smoke-choked air into a chaotic tempest as flames crept ever closer to the terrace's once-elegant decor.

68

Hotel Adlon, Berlin, Germany

Shinkelhof stood before them, *Prometheus* trembling in his unsteady hands. Around him, the battle between Gavrail's forces and Novus raged, bullets slicing through the smoky air, yet he seemed oblivious to the chaos.

"You still don't understand," he whispered, stroking the prototype's lifeless display almost tenderly. "Everything I built... Shinkelhof Medical... from nothing to an empire." His laugh was brittle, like shattered glass. "Twenty years of innovation, of progress. Every breakthrough, every patent, every scientific triumph..."

Dr. Rossi stood on the far side of the terrace, her gaze unyielding and accusatory.

"It was never about money," Shinkelhof continued, his voice thick with emotion. "It was about changing the world. Our medical implants have saved millions of lives. Our neural prosthetics have given the paralyzed the ability to walk again. Every advancement, every innovation..." He faltered, searching for the words. "I built something greater than myself."

Another explosion rocked the building to its foundation. Flames surged rapidly through the upper floors, and the smoke thickened around them, acrid and suffocating.

"We must evacuate, sir!" Dr. Zhang shouted, retreating toward the emergency exit. "The entire structure is about to collapse!"

But Shinkelhof seemed deaf to her plea. His gaze was distant, lost in memories of past triumphs. "When I started the company, I had nothing but a dream. A small basement lab, second-hand equipment... But I saw the potential. I saw the future."

His eyes gleamed feverishly in the firelight. "And now...
Prometheus was supposed to be the crowning achievement. The
ultimate bridge between man and machine. Imagine it—direct
neural interfaces, thought transfer in real time, an entirely new
way to interact with technology..." His voice broke. "It would
have changed everything."

"Battery levels are critical, sir," Dr. Zhang warned. "We can't
stabilize the system much longer."

"An empire built on innovation," Shinkelhof murmured, as if
speaking only to himself. "Every breakthrough, every discovery...
it was my life's work. My vision." He raised *Prometheus* higher,
as though offering it to the heavens. "And now... now it's all
collapsing. Twenty years of work. Thousands of employees.
Millions of patients relying on our products..."

His wide eyes reflected a terrible realization as he watched his
life's work unravel around him. "I just wanted... I just wanted to
create something extraordinary. Something that would change
the world forever."

69

Hotel Adlon, Berlin, Germany

The antique stone tiles of the rooftop terrace vibrated under the pressure of the explosions as dawn gilded Berlin's dramatic skyline. The crown of the historic Hotel Adlon had transformed into an arena for one final, desperate confrontation.

"Behold!" Shinkelhof laughed hysterically, holding Prometheus aloft toward the heavens. "Behold my masterpiece!"

His once-pristine exterior was now utterly undone—his suit in tatters, his eyes fever-bright with madness and realization.

Dr. Rossi took a cautious step forward. "It's over, Reinhart. Put down the prototype. There's no way back now."

"Oh, but it's so much more than that!" His laughter echoed across the terrace, tinged with hysteria. "It's the monument to my hubris! I thought I could own the future through theft... that I could mimic creation by copying the work of others!"

Malaconda stood by the helipad, his aristocratic composure fractured by cold fury. "You're insane, Shinkelhof. This was a simple operation—secure the technology, implement the system. But you... you ruined everything."

"Ruined?" Shinkelhof's voice reached a crescendo. "No, I understood! At last, I understood! It's not about technology—it's about creation, about innovation!" He turned toward the rising sun, his silhouette framed by the inferno below. "We tried to steal the future, and all we grasped was ash!"

A series of explosions rocked the building to its foundations. Flames now consumed the upper floors with terrifying speed, thick smoke rising in choking clouds around them.

"It's time to end this," Malaconda said coldly, raising his pistol.

But Shinkelhof seemed beyond fear. He stood at the edge of the terrace, cradling the lifeless prototype like a sacrificial offering. His eyes burned with a madness that consumed him from within. "I would have changed the world!" he cried to the sky. "I would have created wonders!"

A violent explosion erupted to their right, sending a massive chunk of debris hurtling toward the helicopter circling above. A plume of black smoke burst from its engine as, within seconds, the helicopter veered uncontrollably and plummeted toward the rooftop.

The crashing helicopter struck Shinkelhof in the instant his final outburst reached its peak. In the blinding light of the explosion, they saw his face illuminated with a terrible clarity—the face of a man who finally understood the price of limitless ambition, just before it all ended in fire and smoke.

"I would have been a god..." his last words echoed across the terrace before he vanished into the inferno of metal and flame, the useless prototype falling with him—a final reminder of the price of hubris.

Dr. Rossi remained at the edge, staring down at the devastation below—a silent witness to how dreams of greatness could collapse into nightmares of arrogance and madness.

70

Hotel Adlon, Berlin, Germany

On the ravaged rooftop terrace of Hotel Adlon, Hugo, Sussie, and Dr. Rossi stood amidst the wreckage of what had almost become their undoing. Black pillars of smoke still rose from the smoldering wreckage of the crashed Bell 412 helicopter, while a chorus of police sirens echoed through the city's historic streets. The air felt thin and sterile, like the aftermath of a thunderstorm, carrying a faint tang of ozone and burnt electronics. Scattered remnants of shattered luxury—overturned French designer furniture, broken champagne glasses, torn awnings—bore silent testimony to the violent confrontation.

"Primary area secured," Sussie reported as she methodically scanned the terrain through her tactical binoculars, her professionalism undiminished despite visible exhaustion. "Malaconda escaped in the second vehicle. Nine of the Shadow Council operatives confirmed neutralized; the rest fled northeast. Local authorities are maintaining a perimeter at our directive."

Somewhere in the chaos, Gavrail had vanished as quietly as winter fog. Hugo's gaze turned to Dr. Rossi, standing alone at the terrace's edge, her silhouette stark against the pink hues of the dawn sky. Her face was a mask of pain, and a thick smear of blood covered the lower half of it.

"All of this, for my invention," she murmured, her voice low and fractured. "And someone…" she paused, swallowing hard, "someone gave them access to my original designs. Every detail, every security protocol."

"It's over," Sussie relayed through her still-functioning comms. "Full site cleanup will begin in thirty minutes. All civilian witnesses are under quarantine."

Dr. Rossi reached up to touch her implant, her fingers trembling faintly. The rising sun reflected off her artificial eye—a faint blue glow that served as a subtle reminder that some boundaries, once crossed, could never fully be closed again.

"Beautiful," Sussie whispered suddenly, her gaze fixed on the sunrise over Berlin. "Despite everything... so beautiful."

And no one could tell whether she meant the morning light over the city, or the faintly pulsing blue glow still flickering in Dr. Rossi's eye—a haunting echo of something that was both a promise and a warning of what might yet come.

71

Malmoe, Sweden

Evening light filtered through the tall windows of their apartment in Västra Hamnen, painting the white walls in warm shades of gold and orange. Hugo stood by the large panoramic window with a cup of freshly brewed coffee in his hand— Colombian Supremo, Lita's favorite from the small roastery at Lilla Torg. His reflection in the glass still bore the marks of the Berlin conflict—a healing cut near his temple and a bruise fading from deep purple to yellow.

On his desk lay the latest report from Novus. Madeleine had done an excellent job managing the aftermath of the crisis. Under her leadership, the organization had been restructured to meet the new threats posed by the Shadow Council. Mikko and Sussie had taken charge of a newly formed cybersecurity division, with Freya as their technical lead. Their first major success had been tracing and mapping Malaconda's remaining digital network.

That morning's news broadcasts had covered the dramatic death of Reinhart Shinkelhof. Gavrail remained at large, but with Malaconda's organization in tatters and their Europol connections exposed, his days were numbered. Dr. Rossi had recovered from her injuries and was now working for Novus under strict protection, her expertise safeguarded for the future.

Lita came up behind him with silent steps, wrapping her arms around his waist. The scent of her jasmine shampoo mingled with the rich aroma of his coffee. From the living room, the cheerful laughter of their two-year-old daughter, Elektra, floated in, a sound that never failed to soften Hugo's heart.

"She's missed you," Lita said softly, her voice muffled against his sweater. "Every night, she's asked for her papa, wanting me to tell her stories about how you save the world."

Hugo turned to face her, meeting her warm brown eyes. "What did you tell her when she saw the bandages on my face?"

"That her papa is a hero who protects people," she replied, gently tracing the fading wound near his temple. "She seemed satisfied with that answer. Now she insists on drawing pictures for you every day—her latest masterpiece is hanging on the fridge."

His phone buzzed—a message from Madeleine. Another of Malaconda's cells had been neutralized in Prague. Mikko's team had hacked their communications, while Sussie and Freya had tracked their financial transactions. Novus was evolving into a stronger, more resilient organization, better equipped for the battles ahead. But the deeper investigation into Marcus Thorn's murder had only uncovered more questions, and Hugo knew it would take time to uncover the full truth.

"I'm sorry I scared you," he whispered. "When you heard the news about the hotel... the explosions..."

"Shh," she interrupted, placing a finger on his lips. "I knew what I was signing up for when I married you, Hugo Xavier." She leaned back, her gaze both serious and tender. "You fight for what's right. That's why I love you. Even if it sometimes makes my heart stop."

"Papa!" Elektra's tiny voice interrupted them, and Hugo turned just in time to catch his daughter as she ran toward him on unsteady legs. He lifted her into his arms, and she wrapped hers tightly around his neck, her dark curls the perfect blend of his and Lita's hair.

"Next week," he said, holding his daughter close, "we're going to Copenhagen, all of us. To that playground Elektra loves. Just us three. No Novus, no missions, no secret organizations. Just our family."

Lita's smile grew. "Promise? No surprise phone calls?"

"I promise." He kissed his wife's forehead, then his daughter's cheek. "Some promises are more important than any mission in the world."

They stayed by the window as darkness slowly enveloped the city, a small family huddled together while the lights of Malmö glittered in the twilight. Somewhere out there, Gavrail and the Shadow Council still plotted, weaving their endless intrigues. But for now, in this moment, they were simply Hugo, Lita, and Elektra. And perhaps that was why he fought—to make the world a little safer for the tiny girl in his arms, whose future was worth every battle he could ever fight.

Printed in Great Britain
by Amazon